HUSH MONEY

THE EVERETT BROTHERS SERIES
BOOK TWO

T.D. COLBERT

HUSH MONEY

THE EVERETT BROTHERS SERIES, Book Two

Copyright © 2025 T.D. Colbert

Published: T.D. Colbert 2025

www.tdcolbert.com

Cover Design: Cosmic Letterz

Editing: Jenn Lockwood Editing

To Friend Cassidy & Miss Kerry.

Thanks for loving me like you do.

TRIGGER WARNING

Mentions of infertility, domestic violence, and sexual harassment.

PROLOGUE

TWELVE YEARS AGO - KEATON

"*W*hy do you always order pistachio when you know you don't like it?" Evie asks me as we walk down the boardwalk. I shrug as I shoot her a devious smile then grab her wrist and bring her ice cream to my face, stealing a lick off the side of the cone. She swats me away with a giggle. "Keaton!" she says. I laugh as I lick my lips.

"I just get a kick out of stealing some of yours," I say, veering off the boardwalk and onto the sand. She follows behind, and we both slip our shoes off. It's March and still cool. Seasonal shops are slowly starting to open up, but Coney Island itself is still pretty dead. We're both home for spring break, and I am *really* fucking happy to see her.

College has been rough for me. I have a month and a half left, and then I'm done—thank God.

She's my bright spot, like she always has been— since the third day of freshman year of high school.

But when I got into Stanford, it was a no-brainer that that was where I was going. They had all the programs I wanted. I loved California. And the best part was that it was three thousand miles away from my father.

But Evie...she stayed here in New York. She started at a community college here then finished up her social work degree at NYU so she could commute and keep working. I tried to get her to come out to California with me. She applied to Stanford too—"just for shits and giggles"—and to no one's surprise but hers, she got in. I had long pictured us exploring the West Coast together. I wanted to show her all the things I loved about it. I wanted to get her out of New York, maybe give her a new perspective on herself. Maybe she would see herself the way I saw her. But she said no. She said she had to stay with her family, where she could afford it, where she got the scholarship.

I even offered to pay for her tuition at Stanford out of my trust fund, but she vehemently refused. I was hoping maybe I could change her mind if she could just let go of the stress of the money, if she could just be a college kid. I really needed her. I really *need* her.

When she made up her mind about staying, I offered to pay for her rent in New York so she could move out of her mom's, but she still said no. And even though I was still tempted to do it without her permission, I knew she'd never forgive me if I did it.

I'm not the biggest extrovert, and growing up as an Everett made that pretty difficult. When your father is the third richest man on the planet, it's hard to stay invisible, no matter how hard I have tried. Evie, though...she caught on early. She'd steal the show when the spotlight was on me for too long, or she would suggest leaving campus for lunch or skipping football games when she could tell the noise was getting too loud. She is the best friend I have ever had.

I think it's one of the reasons I fell in love with her when I was fourteen years old. Her knack for reading people is nothing like I've ever seen. She wants to be a social worker, and she will be the absolute best at it. Her empathy knows no bounds, and God, I love her for it.

Like, actually.

I'm in love with my best friend, and I think I have been since the moment we first spoke.

The thing is, she has no idea—or maybe she does. But we've never discussed it. I've been biding my time while we've been apart. She's been enjoying her college years. She wasn't the most social in high school because she always felt out of place. But now, the playing field is a little more even for her. She's made a lot of friends and has finally been letting go of all the weight she carries—at least, a little bit. She goes out to parties, stays with her girlfriends in the city, and has been enjoying her life. Since I can't be there with her to be her escape, I'm glad she is finding her place.

For me, it's been a different story. I'm still the billionaire from New York. Still an Everett, no matter what side of the country I'm on. Finding and sustaining legitimate relationships of any kind is a struggle because even the ones that don't need a friendship with you can still want it for the wrong reasons. So I sort of keep to myself. I've been on a few dates in the past few years, but the truth is, I only see Evie when I look at someone else. It's like drinking out of an empty cup. The only times I've been out in the last four years is when I've flown her out for a visit, and she forced me to. But with her, I don't give a damn where we go. I don't care who is gawking. I don't care who whispers around me. When I'm with her, I'm good.

She's dated a few guys off and on, but much to my pleasure, none of them have lasted very long. One broke up with her because of her closeness to me, claiming she could never feel the way about any other guy that she did about me since I am "a fuckin' billionaire." While I did enjoy being the one who made the other guys jealous, it bothered me at the time that he was claiming it was because of my family fortune. But I know in my heart that Evie has never given a shit about the money or the fame.

I realized how I really felt a few months ago when I had to make a decision on what to do after graduation. I had always thought I'd stay out in California. That I'd find something or start something of my own on the West Coast. Keep my distance from all things Everett.

But the truth is, these few years without her have been impossible. I'm having experiences I always wanted to have, I'm seeing things I always wanted to see, and I'm learning things I wanted to learn, but none of it means a thing without her. She's the first thing I see when I wake up and the last thing I think about before I go to bed. I don't want to be three thousand miles away from her anymore.

She wants to stay in New York. I've always known it was my "duty" since birth to come back and work for the family, and even though I have wanted to resist falling in line, the thought of it doesn't disgust me as much as it used to. As much as I don't mind the physical distance between my father and me, I'd happily see him every day so long as I saw her too.

"So, are you ready?" she asks as I finish spreading the blanket out on the sand, and we take a seat.

"For?" I ask.

"Graduation. Coming back. Being with your dad every week," she says. I sigh as she switches our ice cream cones, finishing off my barely eaten pistachio while I finish her cookies-and-cream.

I shrug.

"Working with him will suck," I say matter-of-factly. "But it'll be good to be with my brothers more often—and you."

She looks up at me, a sheepish smile flashing across her face. Her long strawberry-blonde locks fly around in the wind, and she tucks a strand behind one of her ears. I want to go on.

This is it, Keaton.

You have waited eight years for this.

Tell her.

"So," she says, clapping the crumbs off her hands and turning to me, "I wanted to talk to you about something." My stomach churns.

"Okay," I say, turning to face her. God, she's beautiful. "I'm ready."

"So you know that guy I told you about?" she asks. Now, my stomach sinks. I clear my throat. Yeah, I remember. Some guy she started seeing at the start of the school year. She said it was casual. I don't ask about him. I have never asked about any of them. I just wait until they are out of the picture.

"Tucker?" I ask coyly. She shoots me a look.

"Tanner," she corrects me, both of us knowing damn well that I remembered his name. I nod. "Well, we're still seeing each other. It actually got a little more serious throughout the year." My stomach is churning. It doesn't even feel like butterflies. It feels like...I don't know. Bats? Like rabid bats flying around my stomach. "Well, he actually got a job lined up here in the city when we graduate."

Now my stomach starts twisting.

"Oh, yeah?" I ask, trying to sound casual.

"Yeah," she says. "He's coming into town next month to start looking for places, and...I

think I'm going to go with him. Because...I think we are going to move in together."

There it is.

Quite literally nothing could have prepared me for this.

I saw this day going so, so differently.

I feel all the breath shoot out of my lungs, and my head is spinning.

There's a long, awkward pause as I turn to look out over the ocean.

Then, she breaks it.

"You gonna say anything?" she asks with a nervous giggle. I turn to her and smile.

"I'm happy for you, Eve," I say with the fakest grin in the fucking world. She clears her throat, her eyes dropping down to her hands.

"You're lying to me," she says quietly. I swallow, my eyes darting back out to the sea. It's not a question, and it's not an accusation. It's just a fact.

I clear my throat.

"What do you want me to say, Eve?" I whisper. She clears her throat again.

"I want you to say that you want to meet him," she says. "That you want us to find a place. That you want me to be happy."

I finally get the balls to look up at her.

"I always want you to be happy, Evie, and you know that," I tell her. "But the rest...we've already established that you know when I'm lying. What would be the point?"

And then, I see something that makes my heart start to splinter in my chest.

Tears in her eyes. Caused by me. In all the years we've been friends, I have never once made her cry. And once, when I saw her mom make her cry when we were in high school, I swore to myself that I never would.

"I'm sorry, Eve, I just—"

"Why are you being like this?" she asks me, her lip quivering now. *Fuck me.*

I slide my hand over top of hers, interlocking our fingers and lifting them off the blanket. I bring her hand to my lips and leave a soft kiss on it.

"You know why, Eve," I whisper. She shakes her head, like she doesn't believe me.

"No, I don't," she says. I sigh.

"Evie..." I say.

"But...you've never said anything. You just...I thought..." her voice trails off. She starts to cry, and I pull her into my chest. I stroke her long hair, letting her rest on me like she has so many times before.

God, why was I such an idiot?

"I know," I say, "but I'm saying it now." She pulls back slowly, her green eyes bloodshot and watery. I take in a deep breath. "Evie, you...you're my whole heart. You make my world make sense. I've never really been anyone else's, because I think I've always been yours. And if you want me now, you have me."

More tears well in her eyes as she shakes her head slowly.

"Keat, I...this is a *lot*," she says. I nod. I wait for her to say something—*anything*—else. But she doesn't. A highlight reel plays in my head of every moment, every opportunity I've had over the last eight years to tell her how I felt. And if I could, I'd go back in time to every single one and punch myself in the face for not speaking up.

"If this is what you want," I tell her, "then I want it for you. Because more than anything, I want you to be happy. You deserve the happiness that you bring everyone else, Eve. But I'm not going to stand here and tell you that I want to be a part of it. That *would* be a lie."

She sniffs, and it breaks me even more.

I reach out and bring my hands to her face. I stroke her jawline with my thumb, and I let my eyes roam her freely, trying to commit every corner of her face to my memory in case that's all I have left. Finally, I lean forward and kiss her forehead.

"Evie, no matter what happens, I need you to know that you have me. Always," I say, pushing myself to stand. "Even when you have him, you have me."

You're too late, Keat, I tell myself.

Or maybe—the scariest thought of all creeps in—*maybe I never stood a chance in the first place.*

Present
Day

KEATON

*A*s the wheels of my brother's jet lift off the ground beneath me, I replay the conversation I just had with my brothers over and over and over.

My younger brother, Brooks, and I picked up the call at the same time. I was sitting on the balcony of my perfect apartment in perfect Malibu, figuring out how to save the world in yet another way. Far, far away from New York and anything that would remind me that I am an Everett. My older brother, Julian, was in the office of his Manhattan penthouse. And the idiot that is Brooks? He was lying on a beach somewhere, drinking out of a fucking coconut.

"Do you ever work?" Julian asked him. He laughed and shrugged.

"What's up, J?" I asked, ignoring both of them. My anxiety had been killing me since Julian's girlfriend called us earlier that day to tell us that we needed to answer a call that was going to come in from an unknown number. "Why are you calling us from this number? And why did Sawyer have to tell us?"

"Boys, we're in for it," he told us. "And the only way out is if we're together, and we take down the king."

The king. He meant our father, Cato Everett, the third richest man on the entire fucking planet. The man who gave us everything and never let us forget it. The man who raised us not to take on the world but to boost him higher up, make him look like the loving, doting father and not like the ruthless man who treated our mothers like trash and paid for other people to help parent us.

When everything else in my life went down the drain, I got out of New York as fast as I possibly could. I got to the West Coast and began dedicating my life—and my money—to undoing some of the things my father has spent his life doing. He owns oil; I fund private climate change research and organizations. He buys small businesses to squeeze the juice out of them before hanging them out to dry; I find the ones struggling to keep their doors open and pay their overhead for a year.

I might have his name, but I refuse to be a part of his "legacy."

But now, it appears there is more to this than meets the eye—or the tabloids—with my father. He's done things—terrible things—that he can't undo and that cannot stay buried.

So here I am, on the way back to the very place that broke me.

I close my eyes as the plane lifts higher and higher, leaving my fortress of solitude farther and farther behind.

Getting closer to the fucked-up mess that is my family. The city where I lost everything.

Where I lost *her*.

WHEN THE PLANE FINALLY LANDS, my brother already has a car waiting for me on the tarmac. I recognize the head of my brother's security detail, Russ, and a new guy with him I've never seen before. They both nod in my direction, then Russ wraps me in a big hug and claps me on the back.

"Good to have you in town, Keat," Russ says. Then he stands back and points to the other guy. "This is Mac. He's been training with us for a few months. He will be your detail while you're in town." I roll my eyes and smile. I fucking hate having a security detail. I hate that we think we are so goddamn important that we pay people to follow us around. But my brothers and I are each worth more than the collective wealth of the fucking world. So it's an insurance thing instated by none other than Daddy Dearest.

"Good to meet you, Mac. I'll try to behave while I'm here." I shake his hand, and Russ scoffs.

"So, your brother's place?" Russell asks as we all buckle into the big black Escalade. I think for a second.

I'd love to stop by my favorite Thai restaurant, grab a six pack, and hole up in my apartment in SoHo, hiding away from the world.

But my brother needs me. They both do, even if Brooks is too ignorant to realize it yet. I sigh.

"Yeah. Let's get to Julian's."

WHEN THE ELEVATOR doors open to my brother's penthouse, I take it all in. I don't live like this anymore —at least, not to this extent. I live as much of a minimal lifestyle as possible. Well, as minimal as one can live when they were born into American royalty.

I save most of my money. I invest it in small businesses and non-profits. I try to practice what I preach as much as I can. But when I come back to New York, I get swept back into the glamour of the Everett lifestyle. My big brother, though, works his ass off. He carries the weight of the oldest. The heir to everything, including the brunt of my father's bullshit. Our younger half-brother, Brooks, though... He just reaps the benefits. He lives the exact life that the world thinks we all live—blowing money in a different country every week, surrounded by models and celebrities, wasting away in his warped sense of reality.

But he's about to find out why Julian and I have such a complicated relationship with our father.

Julian rounds the corner, and when he sees me, I see instant relief wash over him. His shoulders fall like he's letting go of some weight, and we wrap each other in a hug. He's probably the person I trust the most in this world. We have been through so much together. The death of our mother. The wrath of our father.

And now this. What's coming now.

Everything has always been on his shoulders. I always feel a little bit better when he feels like he can lay some of it on me.

"Keat," he says, clapping my back. "It's really fucking good to see you."

Around the corner comes in a short brunette, hair cut above her shoulders, wearing one of my brother's sweatshirts. She smiles faintly as she makes her way to me, and I wrap her in a hug too.

"Hi, Keaton," she says.

"Hey, Sawyer," I say back. She's been in my brother's life for a few months now, and honestly, I really like what she's done to him. I've never seen him have the zest he has, the desire to do more for himself and not be so concerned with living up to the expectations laid on him at birth.

"When does Brooks get in?" I ask as we make our way to Julian's living room. Bless his soul, he has takeout from the Thai place waiting for me on the coffee table. He shrugs as he falls into the extra-large couch, Sawyer falling into place beside him.

"Who knows," Julian says. "You know the only sense of urgency that boy has is when it comes to his social life."

I shake my head as I unpack the food, pulling the top off one of the dishes and letting the aroma fill the room. My mouth waters. We sit for a few hours, shooting the shit, talking about the projects I've been working on, talking to Sawyer about the West Coast, and listening to some of the improvements my brother has been making within Everett Enterprises. He really is the best of us. At some point, Brooks texts to say that his jet just landed, and he needs to push till tomorrow.

Typical.

The end of the fucking world as we know it, but Brooksy needs a nap.

After another hour or so, I look up at Julian as Sawyer sleeps quietly in a ball under his arm.

"How bad is this, Julian?" I ask him. He takes a bite of his own food and then looks up at me.

"It's not good, Keat. But if we can pull off what I want to pull off, I think we can save everything." I nod. My big brother always has a plan. "You want to crash here tonight so you don't have to schlep all the way downtown?"

I shake my head as I push to stand.

"Nah. I'm going to get one more night of sleep in ignorant bliss before the world explodes tomorrow."

He smiles and nods.

"Good deal. Mac will get ya home. Be safe. I'll see you tomorrow."

"Night, J," I say as Mac presses the elevator button for me.

. . .

WE DRIVE in silence as we head downtown, the city as loud and bright as ever. But as we go farther and farther down, I sit up.

"Mac, can we make a pitstop?"

Mac nods in the mirror.

"Of course," he says, "you're the boss." I cringe. I hate that. I'm not anyone's boss. I just have the right name. "Where to?"

I look out the window.

I know I shouldn't.

I know it's probably useless anyway.

There is no chance she could still be working there. Right?

"I'll probably be waiting tables here till I'm sixty. You know social workers don't make

shit," she had told me once.

I sigh and swipe a hand down my face.

"Punch in Kim's Diner, please," I tell him. He nods.

And in nine minutes, we're there.

It sits on the corner of an intersection in Midtown, and like just about everywhere else in

New York, there is no convenient parking.

"I'm not supposed to let ya go without me, boss," Mac says. I look at him through the rearview and put a hand on his shoulder.

"Don't call me that. And don't worry. I'm the invisible Everett. I won't be long."

And before he can protest, I open the door and hop out. I open the door, the little bell

ringing, and look around. It's past midnight, but

there are still a few people eating. And then I see her, pouring a cup of coffee for a man sitting at the counter. Her dusty-pink diner shirt and matching apron look like the same one she wore fifteen years ago, and her long blonde locks are pulled back into a messy knot on the top of her head. She smiles as she talks to him, making conversation as easily as ever. She walks down the counter to another customer, clearing her plate and talking to her too. And then her eyes lift to me, and I freeze.

EVIE

*T*he normal diner sounds—the bell chiming, the quiet mutters, the silverware clanking —all seem to cease the second my brain registers that it's him.

Here. In Kim's Diner.

After all these years.

I've thought about this moment so many times. What I would do, how I would react, what I'd say—if anything at all. But then he lays eyes on me, and I completely freeze. I can't move a muscle. My body forgets how to operate, and my brain shuts off.

But then he smiles.

It's faint, and it's pained, but it's beautiful none-theless. And then the little clock that hangs on the wall strikes me back to reality with its ticking, and it's like someone hits the unmute button. I put down the pot of coffee I'm holding and pull my apron off over my head. I walk around the counter and make a beeline for him, still standing just inside the doorway.

I can hear my heart pounding in my ears, and it's not just butterflies in my stomach. It's like a fucking kangaroo in there, bouncing off the goddamn walls. But I just follow my feet straight to him.

"Is it really you?" I ask him as I finally get within inches of him, and his smile widens. Before he answers, he reaches out and pulls me in for the longest, tightest, warmest hug I've had in a decade. It goes on longer than I should let it, but at one a.m., here in Kim's Diner, I really don't give a fuck. My best friend is back.

"Yeah, Eve," he says, his voice leaving a trail of chills on my skin. "It's me." Finally, we come apart, and I just stare up at him for a moment, taking him in. He looks so much the same as he did all those years ago. A little more stubble on his face now, but it makes him look more sophisticated. His eyes are still that striking gray, and I still feel like they see right through me. I notice that he has filled out a little bit; thirty-four-year-old Keaton looks like a man compared to twenty-one-year-old Keaton. He was beautiful then, but he's bigger, stronger now. He looks more... seasoned. But in the best way.

"What...what are you doing here? Are you..."

"Here for you? Yes," he says, and I swallow. "I don't typically make it a habit of hitting up diners at one o'clock in the morning unless it's for good reason." He smiles, and I feel my stomach flip. I clear my throat then pull him toward an open booth at the back of the room. I slip in and motion for him to sit across from me, and thank goodness, he does.

"Well, uh...what are you doing here, Keat? Is everything okay? How did you know I would be here?" I ask.

"I didn't," he admits, leaning back against the booth, the t-shirt he has on tightening over his broad chest. "I was just hoping." My eyes are wide as I wait for him to elaborate. But he doesn't, and I feel myself growing more anxious.

"You were just hoping I'd still be working at the same diner you left me at over a decade ago, huh?" I say with a nervous laugh. But he doesn't smile. His eyes drop to the table as he slides his fingers over the fork that sits on the placemat.

"I didn't leave you," he says, just above a whisper. Then his big gray eyes lift to mine, and I want to punch myself for even letting the words leave my mouth.

You left him, you idiot.

I clear my throat again.

"What are you doing here?" I ask him a second time.

"Just some family stuff," he says awkwardly. "I'm in town for a bit, and uh...I don't know. Just was hoping to see a friendly face."

He's not saying much, but in the same breath, he's saying it all. Well, maybe not *all*. But I know there is more to it. It may have been years, but I still know him.

"What's going on, Keat? Do you want to talk about

it?" I say, and my hand slides over the table and lands on his without me even thinking about it.

Unfortunately for both of us, it's my left hand.

The one where my wedding ring sits.

His eyes lock on the ring.

My eyes lock on his.

And I remember the same look in his eyes eleven years ago when I first told him Tanner was moving to New York. That we were going to move in together. That everything between us—whatever it was—was over as we knew it.

Suddenly, he slides his hand out from under mine and puts it on his lap. Then, he lifts those big, sad eyes to me.

"Nah," he says. "I'm good. I should get going, but it was good to see your face, Evie Rae." With that, he slides out from the table, out of the diner, and seemingly, back out of my life. And then I'm just sitting in this booth, the dark-red pleather sticking to my thighs, wondering what the absolute fuck just happened.

MY SHIFT finally ends a little while later, and I am completely numb the entire way back out to Long Island. When I work late nights at the diner, I drive into the city. I like having the time to myself to think. To be at peace.

Because then, I get home. And the peace is gone.

The eggshells are back, and I tiptoe across them as gracefully as I can...but sometimes I walk too heavy.

As I pull into our driveway, my mind is consumed by another complicated man.

Why is he back? Why did he come find me?

A million thoughts swirl around my head.

Is something wrong? Is he here for good? Is someone sick? Is *he* sick?

But then I'm jolted back to reality the second I realize the living room light is on in my house.

Our house.

He never leaves the light on for me.

Which means he's awake. After he's been out drinking with his friends all night.

Not a good combination. I draw in a long breath and blow it out slowly.

I grab my purse and walk to the door. I go to unlock it, but it pushes open. I walk inside and set my keys down on the entry table and kick my shoes off under the entryway bench. I used to love this house. It's a cute little Cape Cod, painted a metal blue with white trim and shutters.

It used to feel like a breath of fresh air. Like something I put my mark on. Like somewhere we were setting roots and growing our lives.

Now it feels more like the place where I hold my breath. Like when I walk through the door, I'm diving under water.

I round the corner into the living room and jump when I see Tanner sitting in one of the armchairs. He's facing the door, but he's not looking at me. He's swirling a glass of whiskey around, staring at it. Finally, he lifts his brown eyes to me, and there's a darkness to them that I haven't seen in a while.

I'm not sure what it is—maybe it's the way his eyes fix on me, like he's stalking prey, or the way his face shows no emotion—but the hairs on the back of my neck stand up.

"Where were you?" he says. I give him a look and cock my head.

"I was at the diner," I say. "You know where I was." He widens his eyes and takes another sip. He finishes it off then looks at the empty glass for a minute. Then he looks back to me.

"Who were you with?" he asks. I swallow.

"A lot of people. My coworkers, the regular night shifters." He nods.

"Anyone else?"

Fuck. Why is he asking this?

Something doesn't feel right.

Something feels...dangerous. The way he's looking at me. The way everything feels too quiet, like the calm before a storm. Something inside of me is screaming to do something. *Anything.*

I take in a breath and pull my purse off over my head. I walk it around the corner and slide my phone out of the pocket. I don't know what pushes me to do it, but I open up a text to the only other person I know who is awake at this hour. And the only person who may read more into it—and act.

I open a text to Keaton and send him my location, praying it's still his number. Then I turn around to walk back into the living room, but I let out a little scream when I almost crash into Tanner. He's hovering over me, his shirt disheveled, and the alcohol oozing out of his pores. I take a small step back.

"I asked you a question," he growls, gritting his teeth. I swallow.

"An old friend stopped by the diner," I say. "Remember, uh...my friend Keaton?"

He takes a step toward me, and I back up.

"Yeah. I remember you talking about him. But what I don't remember is you telling me you two were still chummy. And I don't remember you telling me why the *fuck* he was in the diner you work at at one in the fucking morning."

He takes another step, and I feel myself press up against the wall. I swallow as he closes in on me.

Keaton once told me that he'd do anything for me.

God, I hope that's still true.

KEATON

Twenty minutes ago, I was sitting in the big leather chair in the living room of my Manhattan apartment that I never visit, holding a glass of whiskey that I never drink.

I was contemplating everything.

My life. The future of my family and our business.

The decision I made all those years ago to leave and never look back.

But now, I'm in the back of one of the company's Escalades, flying down I-495 out to Long Island.

I don't know why. Maybe it was an accident. Or maybe it was an S.O.S. I want to call her, but I don't know what's going on. I am afraid to make the situation—if there is one—any worse. And I won't be able to rest until I know which one.

Luckily, at this time of night, we're not hitting a whole lot of traffic. And we get into the little Long

Island town she sent me in under forty minutes. I'm just praying that it's not forty minutes too late.

When we turn onto the street, I look down at the GPS on my phone.

"It's that one," I tell Mac, and he makes the right turn into the driveway. It's a charming little house, but I don't have much time to admire it. I open the door before he even puts the car in park, and when my feet touch the ground, so do his. I hold up my hand to him, and he gives me a look.

"Boss, don't get me fired on my first solo night," he pleads. "I'm supposed to have your six everywhere."

"Follow me, but don't make a sound," I tell him. He nods.

She's married. I saw the ring. She's probably inside with her husband. I sneak up the front walk toward the front door. A light is on inside, but I can't see anything through the blinds on the window. I wait a beat but don't see anything. I let out a sigh. Maybe it was a false alarm. She probably doesn't even realize she texted me. And as much as I hate the fact that she's inside with her *husband,* there is a part of me that's relieved. I turn on my heel, motioning for Mac to go back to the car, just as I hear glass shattering. And then I hear the sound that makes my blood run cold: her scream.

I lunge for the front door, turning the handle frantically, but it's locked. I don't wait. I just start banging. I feel Mac next to me. I see his hand reach for his hip.

But as the door bursts open, I hold my hand out to him. If I can help it, I won't have a gun around her.

When the door opens, I see a sweaty, brooding man with dirty blond hair out of place, his shirt undone, and whiskey on his breath. *Tanner.* His eyes are on fire, and when he sees me, they don't seem to dim much. I follow his other hand, which is wrapped tightly—too tightly—around Evie's wrist. I grit my teeth.

You can't kill him. You can't kill him.

"Who the fuck are—" Tanner starts, but I push inside the house, Mac right behind me. Now we're chest to chest, and while we are close, I've got about a half inch on him. And I'm using it. I reach around him without taking my eyes from his and unlatch his slimy fingers from her arm, tugging her gently around him to me. I pull her behind me slightly, then I motion to Mac to step in. He does, and I turn to her. I inspect her up and down. I don't see any blood or marks, with the exception of the indentations of his fingers on her arm. I rub it gently then meet her eyes.

"Are you okay?" I ask. She nods, tears in her eyes, and bites her lip.

"You came," she whispers. And it's taking every-thing inside of me not to scoop her up and run out of the house.

I squeeze her hand then look at her.

"Go pack a bag," I tell her. Her eyes widen, and she moves them slowly from me to him. "You're coming with me tonight, Eve," I say. I don't say it like a question, because it's not. There's no fucking way I'm leaving here tonight without her. She nods and slips out from my shadow and walks up the stairs. I hear a scoff from behind me as he turns toward the steps.

"Your ass ain't going anywhere, Evie," Tanner calls up the stairs. He starts to turn toward the steps, but Mac puts a hand to his chest. Tanner's eyes drop to it before he shakes him off. In a minute's time, she's back down the stairs with a small duffel. Then she shakily walks toward me. Tanner turns to me as I grit my teeth.

"Don't even think about it," Tanner says in her direction, and I feel my fists clench at my sides. But I let it go. I slip the bag off her shoulder and put it on mine, guiding her toward the door. "Evie. *Evie!*" he screams, and I see her shoulders jump. I can't stand watching the reaction she has to him. I spin on my heel so that we're face to face again, and I feel her grip my sleeve. "I don't know who the *fuck* you think you are, but—"

"My name is Keaton Everett," I say, and I watch his eyes turn to saucers as he puts it together. Out of respect for me, Evie didn't tell many people that she was best friends with an Everett. I guess that includes her husband. "I am leaving, and she is coming with me. Unless she reaches out to you, do not contact her."

He scoffs.

"You think you can just walk into *my* house and take my *wife?* My fuckin' *wife?*"

I smile.

"I'm not taking her. She's leaving on her own. And there's not a damn thing you can do about it."

He takes a wobbly step toward us, and again, I can feel her tense up.

"You sure about that?" he says. I feel Mac tense up too, but again, I hold my hand out. I step toward Keaton.

"Oh, I'm positive. Do you know why?" I ask. I *hate* where I come from. I hate nepotism. I hate the perks. I resent everything that has to do with the Everett name. I've never used it—until right now. "I will buy the company you work for, and I will fire you from it. Then I'll buy your house and your cars at auction. I'll sue you for whatever Everett Enterprises' legal team comes up with. And if you ever, *ever* put a hand on her again, I'll fucking kill you. I'll call the police myself, and I'll smile the whole way to the fucking cell. And I'll sleep like a fucking baby."

He swallows, and I should be embarrassed about how pleased I am with myself. But I'm not.

Then, I spin on my heel and guide her out the door. Mac waits for us to get to the car before he leaves the porch, and before I know it, we're backing out of the driveway and pulling out of their neighborhood.

She is shaking in the seat next to me, and I reach out and wrap my arm around her shoulder and the other under her legs. I lift her off her seat and onto my lap, cradling her like a baby while she sobs quietly into my shirt.

Her whole world just quaked before her eyes.

Holding her like this shouldn't feel this good.

But it does.

A LITTLE WHILE LATER, Mac is pulling into the garage underneath my building. She's calmed down some, her eyes red and puffy. Mac opens our door, and I let her slide out first. He helps her out, and I grab her bag. I hike it over one shoulder then take her by the hand. We get in the elevator, and Mac scans a key fob that brings us up to my floor. It's not a penthouse like my brother, but it's nothing to laugh at. It's still a four-bedroom apartment with panoramic views of the city I had so much disdain for. But it's not flashy enough to make me stick out from the rest of the New York elite.

But as Mac opens the door to my apartment, and I see the shining lights of the city that's still wide awake, I realize maybe I don't hate it so much after all. It's the city that gave me her.

We get safely inside, and after Mac does a sweep, he posts up in my study. I take her hand and lead her down the long maze of a hallway to where my suite and the other primary suite sit. I open the door to the guest room and lead her inside. I put her bag down on the dresser and turn on some lights. I look around.

This room—scratch that—this entire apartment could really use some TLC. I never did much in the way of decorating. It's more of a safe place for me to land whenever I have business here. But I never wanted to make it too inviting, because I never wanted to stay.

But seeing her here in this bleak, cold, all-white room, I wish it felt more like a second home and a little less like a mental hospital. I turn to her, and she looks like a shell of the girl I once called my best friend. She feels so small right now, bundled up in an oversized sweatshirt, her ponytail loose on her shoulder, her strawberry-blonde hair falling out of place. I take a step toward her, and she lifts her big green eyes to me.

I know her mind is racing a million miles per minute. I know she's thinking of all the things she has to take care of, decide, handle. But I'm going to put a stop to that—at least for tonight.

I take a step toward her, and I reach my hands out to her arms, tugging her gently into me. I pull her head to my chest and cradle it while my other hand rubs her back.

"Not tonight," I whisper. Her eyes jump to mine, confused. "No more thinking tonight. Just sit here with me in this apartment. Safe. You can think again tomorrow."

Her eyes go wide like saucers, and she nods.

"Tomorrow," she whispers.

EVIE

*I*t shouldn't feel this good.

With everything that's going on in my life right now—most of which has transpired in the last hour—the last thing I should be doing is curling up against my on-again-off-again ex-best friend. But here I am.

And it feels *good*.

He's warm. He's sturdy. And right now, he's just quiet. We're just sitting in silence on this big brown couch that feels like it's fresh off the showroom floor, and I wonder how many times someone has sat on it. There are no photos on the walls, no plants, no nothing that insinuates signs of life. Some random paintings hang on the walls but nothing that feels like Keaton.

But I decide not to ask tonight.

I decide to just let this go on as long as it can.

I curl up tighter against him as he flicks through

the channels. Then I see him scroll back up to *Three's Company*, and I turn my chin up to him.

"No way," I say with a shy smile. He smirks.

"It's always on this time of night," he says.

"It is?" I ask, surprised that he knows this.

"Yep," he says. "I watch it almost every night."

"You do?" I ask. He smiles.

"Yeah. It reminds me of my best friend."

I swallow as I stare up at him.

His best friend.

I sit up and turn toward him, crossing my legs underneath me and facing him.

"What made you come tonight?" I ask him.

"What do you mean? You sent me your location."

"I know," I say. "But I..." my voice trails off. He turns to me and puts his hand on top of

mine.

"Eve, if I sent you my location, what would you have done?"

I think for a moment. I would be anxious. I would overthink it a million times. But I know what I would do.

"I would come," I say. He nods.

"Exactly," he says.

"But even after..." my voice trails off again. I'm not really sure what I need him to say. I just want to know why, after the way we left everything, he still came. He brought me back here. He's still sitting with me now.

"Even after," he says. His eyes drop down to our now

intertwined fingers for a moment. "Eve, I told you years ago that you will always have me. *Always.* And I meant it. Even when you had him, you had me. *Have* me."

I force myself to look up at him, and I can feel the tears burning in the backs of my eyes. What could I have done to deserve those words?

We sit in silence for a minute before he pushes to his feet.

"I'll grab you a towel. The guest room is all yours," he says quietly. But as he turns to go, I reach up and grab his sleeve. He looks down at me, his eyebrows knit together.

"I, uh...I don't..." I try to say. "I don't..."

I don't know how to tell my maybe-not-ex-best friend that I don't want to sleep by myself. Because after everything he just did for me, the last thing I should be doing is asking him for something—particularly something that sends a million other confusing mixed signals. And my signals are so crossed I don't even know what I'm sending out.

He doesn't say anything. He just pats my hand and walks away, headed down the hallway toward the bedrooms.

Fuck. I wish I wasn't such a fucking lunatic sometimes. After more than a decade, he answered my vague S.O.S., he drove across town, rescued me from my own house and husband, and gave me shelter and a literal shoulder to lean on. And now I want him to... what? Read me a bedtime story? Cuddle?

He could have a girlfriend for all I know. I've been a tad preoccupied with my own shit. I have no idea—

Just as I'm about to spiral off into a ruthless game of "what-if," he returns from the dark hallway. He has a large comforter in his hand and two pillows. He throws one down on one end of the couch and the other on the opposite end. He opens the blanket and spreads it out over me and the other end of the couch, and then he sits down on the other end and pulls it over himself.

He's sleeping out here with me.

He won't even suggest a bed—for a number of very important reasons.

But he knows I don't want to be alone.

So we're sharing the couch.

He's not leaving.

I settle down into my nook of the couch, laying my head on the ultra-comfy foam pillow he brought out for me. The pillowcase smells like fresh linen, and as I breathe it in, I realize how exhausted I am.

I start to let myself get sleepy when thoughts of Tanner start to descend.

The look in his eyes when he asked me about Keaton.

The way he blocked the doorways to control where I could move in the house.

The hole he punched in the drywall.

The glass bowl we got as a wedding gift, shattered on the floor.

The grip he had on my wrist.

I don't even realize that my leg is jumping with anxiety until Keaton slides his hand over my thigh, gripping it lightly. It sends a shock through my body, both a zap to reality and a jolt of energy that goes right to my core.

"I'm right here, Eve," he whispers in the dark. I nod, sliding my hand down to his. Our fingers lock, and my brain starts to quiet.

I don't know what tomorrow brings. But I remember what he said earlier.

Not tonight.

Tomorrow.

KEATON

I should move.

I should get up and move.

I should untangle her legs from mine.

I should free my sweatpants from the death grip she's had on the fabric since she finally fell asleep last night.

But I'm not going to. Because watching her sleep in *my* apartment, on *my* couch is bringing me a sort of peace that I never thought I'd experience again. I know it might be short-lived. I know it will *most likely* be short-lived. All the more reason for me to soak in every second of it.

God, she's even more beautiful than she was when we were kids. The thirties version of Evie is my favorite. There was something missing in her big green eyes, though, when I saw her in that diner earlier. All our lives, she was the most self-assured, steadfast person I had ever known. She kept me grounded.

Now, though, she seems like she questions every move she makes.

Like she might need someone to remind her who she is.

God, I want it to be me.

And as I watch her draw in a long, shuddered breath, I realize that I'm right back to where I was a decade ago.

Completely in love with her.

Fuck.

SHE STIRS AGAIN, finally loosening her grip, and I decide to sneak out from under her and make some coffee for when she does wake up. I pad across the living room and into the kitchen, flick the espresso machine on, and get to work. While I wait for it to brew, I steal another look at her, her hands now folded up underneath her face. I don't know what it will mean when she wakes up, but if this is all I get, then I want to remember every second of it.

Just as I'm stirring two Sweet-n-Lows into her cup and adding "absolutely no cream" as she would have ordered it ten years ago, I wonder if her order has changed. I wonder if any of her other tastes have changed too.

"Morning," I hear her murmur behind me as I'm spinning back around to face her, one mug in each hand. She's sitting up on the couch now, rubbing her eyes and tucking a stray lock of copper hair behind her ear. I can't help but smile. The light streams in from all the windows, and she's glowing.

"Morning," I say, walking toward her and holding one of the mugs out to her. She inspects it then smiles.

"Absolutely no cream?" she asks. I smile and nod as I sit back down next to her.

"Not a drop," I assure her. "Wasn't sure if you still took it like that, but I figured I'd give it a shot."

She takes a sip and smiles.

"I'm a creature of habit," she says. "Not much has changed."

There's an awkward silence between us, and I'm pretty sure we're both thinking the same thing.

Everything has changed.

"What are—"

"Why are—" we both go to speak at the same time. She smiles.

"You go," she says. But I shake my head. "Okay, um...I was just gonna ask why you were back in New York. Or, I guess, how often you come back?"

I put my mug down on the coffee table and look at her.

"Not often," I say. "New York is...hard for me." She swallows and looks down at her cup. "But there's some shit going on with the uh...businesses. And J called and asked me to come, so I did."

She nods.

"Anything you want to talk about?" she asks. I can't help but smile. Her world is literally flipping on its axis, but she wants to talk about me. I shake my head and put my hand over top of hers.

"Yeah," I say. "You." She lifts her eyes to mine. "Talk to me, Eve."

Her eyes drop immediately, and I see her hands sneak out from under mine and immediately start twisting the fringe on the blanket. I put my hands on hers again. I wait for her to slow down a beat and raise those big emerald blues to me again. And then I see the tears forming in them, and it takes everything in me not to reach out and pull her into me.

"What am I gonna do?" she whispers, and her voice cracks under a soft sob. She swallows it back down, but I can see her fighting it off. We sit in silence for a moment as I get my bearings and figure out how I'm going to respond to that. A good friend would tell her she would figure it out. That she will make the right choice. That she'll get back on her feet.

But if I learned anything over the last twenty years of having her in and out of my life, it's that I don't want to be her friend.

And I want her to know that nothing has changed about the way I feel for her.

That she's too good for a life where she's afraid in her own home.

I stroke the back of her hand with my thumb, and I look into her eyes.

"You're going to leave him, Eve," I say just above a whisper. Her eyes widen and flit up to mine. I feel her palm clamming up under mine.

"I...I can't afford to leave him," she says. "It's not that—"

"Whatever you need is yours," I tell her, and she slips her hand out from under mine, shaking her head like a maniac.

"No. Absolutely not." She stands up, wrapping her arms around her body and walking toward the huge windows that look out over the city. It's rainy today, and despite the crisis she's having, I just want to wrap her up and carry her to my bed, stay cooped up all day, and ignore any and all of the responsibilities that we both wish would vanish into thin air.

I stand slowly, walking leisurely toward her. I get closer until my chest is only an inch or two from her back. I lower my head down so my lips are next to her ear.

"I told you, Evie," I whisper. "Even when you had him, you still had me. And you still do."

EVIE

My heart is pounding so hard in my chest right now that I'm pretty sure I have completely forgotten how to breathe. It feels like my throat is closing every time I try to breathe in.

Tanner.

The drinking.

Keaton.

The money.

Him.

It all feels like way too much right now, and I don't know what to do about it. I don't know how to do anything. What I *want* to do is sink back into him. Let him hold me up. Let him carry me through this apartment and throw me onto that big ol' bed of his like a rag doll.

But clearer heads must prevail.

In all the years I've known him, I have prided myself on being the one person in his life who didn't care about who he was or what he had to offer. It was always a joke, even when we were kids, that I would never let him pay for anything. I'd find places for us to hang out where we would be the least likely to be seen. Where no one would realize who he was. Where we could just *be.*

So this? Him suggesting I let him fund my *divorce?* And ten years after I'm pretty sure I ripped his heart out of his chest, no less.

No.

I won't do it.

I can't do it.

I wrap my arms tighter around my body. But when he steps even closer and I feel his warmth, all that *independent woman* stuff goes to shit. Because I let myself lean back on him, and he slowly snakes his arms around me.

"You have whatever you need," he says again, and I squeeze my eyes shut, shaking my head back and forth on his chest.

"No," I say again.

But he just squeezes me tighter.

"Yes," he fights back.

"Why?" I ask after a moment. When he doesn't answer, I turn so we're face to face. "Why would you even...why are you doing this?" He reaches out and locks our hands together again.

"Because you deserve everything you want in life, Evie. And what I saw last night...that can't be it."

I wriggle free from his grasp and take a few steps.

"How do you know?" I ask him. "How do you know you didn't just catch us on a bad night?"

He cocks his head and takes a step toward me.

"Did I?" he asks simply. "Do you normally send out distress signals on your 'bad nights'?" I swallow. The truth is, no. Because I never had anyone around that I thought might actually answer them.

I don't answer him. I just bite my bottom lip. He takes another step toward me.

"Is it like that a lot, Evie?" he asks. I swallow again. I wish I could say no. But he'd know I was lying. I nod slowly. "Has he..." He pauses for a moment, draws in a breath, then lifts his eyes to me. "Has he hurt you?" he asks through gritted teeth.

I shake my head no slowly.

"No," I say.

A see a flash of relief wash over his face.

"But you've thought he might?" he asks. I pick up a lock of my hair and begin to twirl it. Then I nod. He steps closer to me and takes my hand. He brings it to his lips. "That's too much, Eve. Too close."

I swallow.

I know he's right.

I know this is too much.

I know that whatever there is between Tanner and me, it hasn't resembled love in a very long time.

I know that the last time I tried to initiate sex, he drunkenly told me that I had gotten a little "soft around the middle" before he passed out.

I haven't tried since.

That was ten months ago.

I know that I take more and more shifts at the diner each month so that I can be home less. I know that, for the past year, when our friends have asked us to get together, we have both made up numerous excuses.

I know that the numerous times I asked him to go to couples therapy, he spat on the idea and told me that was "crazy-people shit."

And I know that I feel happiest when I'm alone and the most tense when I'm with him.

And I know that, over the last few months, I have started to feel *scared* in my own home. My mind has wondered about how far he might go the next time.

Too much.

I feel my eyes burning, and when I lift them to Keaton, the tears flow out of them. He takes the last few steps toward me and pulls me into him again. And then I let myself cry again. I don't know for how long, but he doesn't seem to care. When I finally pull myself out of it, I wipe my eyes and look up at him.

"Okay," I finally say.

He raises an eyebrow.

"Okay?" he asks. I nod. He squeezes my shoulders. "Does your, uh...family know what's

been going on?"

My eyes grow wide as the reality of this decision I'm making sets in. I walk slowly toward the couch again, slapping a hand to my face.

"Oh, god," I say. "My family. His family. My shit... *fuck.*"

He follows me back to the couch, sitting on the coffee table in front of me.

"Don't worry about your family," he says. He knows about my family. He knows they were nothing but stress for me as a kid and a young adult. He knows that I could never lean on them, and that hasn't changed. "You will stay here. For as long as you want. Okay?"

I suck in a slow breath.

I nod. He nods.

"Okay," he says. "When do you work next?"

I think for a moment.

"I work at the diner tomorrow night. Then the office Monday through Friday."

He cocks his eyebrow again.

"Office?"

"I work for the state. I'm a social worker," I say. A small smile creeps over his perfect lips. "What?"

He shakes his head.

"Just always knew you'd be what you said you'd be. And I know you're fucking amazing at it."

I bite my lip.

"Okay," he goes on, "I'm going to have one of our security guys bring you to and from work." My eyes grow wide again. "It's just precautionary. But that way, we know you're safe. They will bring you to work, here, and anywhere else you want to go. I won't tell anyone you're here, if you don't want me to. Take the time you need. You can breathe while you are figuring everything else out."

I swallow.

Everything else.

Like my whole fucking life.

I nod.

"Thank you, Keat," I whisper.

"I'd do anything for you, Eve," he says with a smirk. He pats his lap then stands up from the table. "I have to meet my brothers soon, so I'm gonna shower. The kitchen is stocked, or feel free to order whatever you want for delivery."

I nod and force a smile, but he sees through it. He bends down so our eyes are locked.

"You're gonna be okay, Evie Rae Dawson," he says with a wink. "I promise." Then he bends down to leave a long, slow kiss on my forehead before turning on his heel and walking down the hall.

Evie Rae Dawson.

I'll never forget the first time he called me Evie.

Twenty Years Ago

EVIE

"Genevieve Dawson," Mr. McNeil calls out. I shudder internally.

I raise my hand.

"Here," I mutter quietly. He marks me as present and keeps moving with the rest of the attendance. It's my first day of high school, and I thought I felt out of place in middle school. But getting an academic scholarship to the ultra-expensive prep school where all of Manhattan's richest kids go? That takes the cake. I saved up all my wages from working at the frozen yogurt place all summer so I could buy a few t-shirts and a single pair of jeans from Hollister, just in case I make some friends who want to hang out outside of school.

I'm thankful we all have to wear these stupid uniforms so that at least my non-designer clothes don't give me away as a fraud.

I'm ahead of my grade level in just about every

subject, and my advisor suggested I take a few classes over the summer so I could be even more ahead. I'm in advanced world history right now, and there is only one other freshman in this class.

And he happens to not only be the richest kid in Manhattan, but an Everett.

Which makes him a member of one of the wealthiest families on the entire planet.

A lot of the kids in class seem highly interested in that. They surround his desk, talking to him about his family, their compound, his dad. But I just sit at my desk. Money doesn't impress me, because most of the people I know who have it don't tend to share. They don't use it for the good of those around them. So it doesn't really change much.

There are a lot of famously rich kids at this school —sons and daughters of celebrities and politicians. It's like nepotism runs through the dang water fountains.

But going here gives me a much better shot at getting an academic scholarship for college. And if I don't get that, I don't go.

So I'll suck it up for the next four years.

I'll try and stay as invisible as I can.

Being alone isn't scary to me. I'm alone a lot. Even at home. Even when the house is full, I'm still on my own a lot. My parents divorced when I was young, and I don't see my dad a lot. My older brother moved up to Boston before I was even in middle school, and my mom works a lot.

The only person who genuinely enjoys my company is my Nanny. Her apartment is about three blocks from ours, and I probably spend more time there than I do at ours.

When she's not home, I spend most of my time by myself. I read a lot. I walk around the city. I go to museums.

I learned at a young age that it was better to spend time by myself than be around the people who made me wish I was.

Like my mom.

My mom didn't ask for the life she has.

My dad had a good job. His family had money. She thought she would always have that. But when they divorced, she had to go back to work. And when ends weren't meeting, she had to take a part-time job too. It's not hard to see that she resents me. She criticizes my hobbies and interests and is constantly pushing me to look into "more lucrative" career plans. Like I knew what "lucrative" meant in eighth grade. While my friends were dreaming of being fashion designers or professional athletes, she was pushing me to look into sales or engineering.

And when I told her I didn't want to, she rolled her eyes.

Starting at the end of sophomore year, I get to pick a career track and choose my elective classes based off of that. I haven't told her yet, but I am really interested in sociology or psychology.

People interest me.

She just doesn't realize that, because I don't interest her.

My next few classes whizz by, and my planner is already jam-packed with deadlines and due dates. I pull my school map out of my notebook as discreetly as possible to remind myself how to get to the cafeteria. This school is a damn maze.

"B Lunch?" a voice asks from behind me, making me jump.

I turn around to see him staring back at me. The Everett kid. I swallow and look around. He's got to be talking to someone else. He raises an eyebrow. "Genevieve, right?" I bite my lip.

Guess not.

I nod slowly.

"Y-yeah," I stammer. "And you are..." Sweet Lord. I don't know his first name. I know his dad is Cato Everett. I know his older brother is Julian.

But I can't remember his fucking name, and he knows mine.

How ironic.

I feel heat flush my cheeks, and he smiles.

"Keaton," he says, sticking a hand out to shake mine. I move my books over to my other arm and take his. I smile shyly.

"It's nice to meet you—officially," I say with a curt nod. "And yes, B Lunch. I just have no idea how to get to the damn cafeteria. This building is stupid big."

He laughs.

"It is," he says. "I am going to go out for lunch. Do

you want to tag along?" he asks, nodding toward a tall man standing by the side door of the building, dressed in a black polo and slacks. And as I look at him, I realize it's his security.

I think about it for a second.

Probably not smart to get in cars with strangers, but I imagine my mom would be happier about me getting into a car driven by an adult security guard than another teenager. And getting out of this stuffy building for a little bit sounds a lot better than cramming into a busy cafeteria with hundreds of people who either don't notice me or pretend they don't.

"Sure," I say with a shrug. He slings his bag over his shoulder, and we walk toward the doors. The man gets the door for us and leads us to the side of the building where a black SUV is parked next to the sidewalk.

As we walk through the courtyard toward it, I freeze when I see a large metal plaque that hangs over the garden.

"'Everett Garden,'" I read, making the connection. Our eyes lock, and he rolls his lips together. He runs a hand down the back of his perfectly tousled sandy locks.

"Uh, yeah," he says. "My great-grandfather sort of built the school."

My eyes widen.

"Sort of?" I ask as the man in the suit opens the car door for us.

He smiles and shrugs, waiting for me to slide in.

We drive a little ways off campus, and I meticulously check my watch. I have class in exactly fifty-three minutes, and if I'm not ten minutes early, I will feel like I'm late. I don't want to come off as stuffy or stuck-up, but I don't imagine that the kid whose name is on the damn school has to adhere to the same rules as the rest of us—particularly those of us whose parents don't make hefty donations each year.

"We will be back before sixth period," he says, and I look up at him. He isn't saying it in a mocking way. He's smiling, but he's not laughing at me. I think he can just tell that I'm anxious about it. "Promise," he adds with a wink, and I feel my stomach flip.

A few minutes later, we park, and he slides out, holding the door open for me to get out. I follow behind him and realize he's headed for a taco truck. I smile. Wouldn't have pegged him for a food truck guy.

As we approach, he says good afternoon to the owner and then places his order. He turns to me.

"Know what you want?" he says. I step forward. Everything looks delicious.

"I'll just do two chicken tacos, please," I say, but then I become conscious of the fact that he's reaching for his wallet. I reach into my bag and yank mine out, pulling a wad of cash out and slapping it on the counter. The man looks at both of us with a peculiar look, but before Keaton can protest, the man slides the cash away.

"Why did you do that?" he asks me, his tone soft and curious.

I shrug.

"I don't need you to pay for me," I say.

He just stares back at me for a second, eyes wide. Then he narrows them on me, nodding slowly. A few minutes later, we're sitting on a park bench, eating the tacos that I just bought for us.

"Did you grow up around here, Genevieve?" he asks. I nod slowly as I finish my bite, wiping my face with a napkin. "What was that?" he asks.

I look at him.

"What was what?"

"That face you just made," he says. "Did I strike a nerve?"

I cringe. Sometimes my face is louder than I intend on it being.

"Oh, sorry, nothing," I say. He turns his whole body to me.

"No, no," he says with a boyish smile. "What was that? Something I said?"

I smile and sigh.

"Yeah, actually," I say. "My name."

"Your...your name?" he asks, one eyebrow raised.

I nod.

"I sort of...hate it."

He chuckles.

"You hate your name?" he asks. But when he sees that my expression hasn't changed, he grows a little more serious.

"I, uh...I don't know. I guess it just carries some

not-so-fun baggage with it. It just...it never felt like it fit me."

I wait for him to ask me more questions. But instead, he just looks at me. His eyes look over my face so much that I start to feel a little self-conscious—as if sitting with a billionaire fifteen-year-old boy doesn't do that enough already.

"Okay," he says, leaning back and putting his arm on the back of the bench. "What can I call you, then?"

I look at him. That's it? No interrogation? No nothing?

I swallow.

"Umm...Evie," I say, tucking a piece of hair behind my hair. "It's what my Nan calls me. She's the only one who does. My mom says it's childish. She says Genevieve carries a little more, I don't know...serious-ness...to it. But I don't much care. Evie is really the only name that ever made me feel like me. But my mom refuses to call me anything but Genevieve."

He thinks for a minute, his lips moving from side to side. Then, he sticks out his hand to me.

"It's nice to meet you, Evie," he says with a smile. I can't help but smile back as I take it. "Now, let's get you back for sixth period."

Present Day

KEATON

I turn the shower on hot then double back to turn the dial down. I know she's going through the wringer right now, but *God,* she's so fucking beautiful. And this close proximity, those big green eyes, the way she is in distress but still stays so kind...*fuck.* And the way her hair still smells the same. The way she smiles at me. The way she makes me feel like she needs me.

Apparently, my cock thinks I'm fifteen again. The way I have had to position myself is embarrassing.

I swipe a hand down my face.

Get it together. She's struggling, you dick.

I stare at my face in the mirror.

I have always been the odd one out, looks-wise, despite Brooks only being our half-brother.

I have gray eyes, unlike both of my brothers' deep-brown ones. I also got my mom's sandy hair rather than their dark-brown locks. Lately, when I look at my reflection, I feel *old*. I see an unfulfilled, jaded man looking back at me.

But right now, I see something in my own eyes that I haven't in a really long time: hope. And that's a beautiful, scary thing. I have to remind myself that she had the chance to be with me before, and she didn't take it.

I have to remind myself that she chose *him*.

I have to remind myself that she's vulnerable, and lost, and not in a good place.

But I can't seem to remember any of that any time she's looked at me over the last twenty-four hours.

All I see is her.

I get into the cold shower and swipe a hand over my face. I almost laugh as I look down at my raging hard-on.

Fuck me.

AFTER MY VERY LONG, very cold shower that didn't stop me from coming twice while thinking about her, I get dressed and make my way back out into the living room. I expect to see her, but she's gone. I look around, walking down the halls, until I find the door to the study open. I walk toward the open door and peek inside. I see her, wrapped in the same blanket we slept under last night, staring down at a frame on the desk. I swallow audibly when I realize what picture she's looking at.

She lifts her eyes to me from across the room.

"You...you kept this?" she asks.

Without even looking back down at the picture, I nod, walking toward her and picking it up. I smile when I look at it. I can't even help it.

"Always," I say, setting it back down. It's a photo of us at our high school graduation. She's on my back, holding her cap in one hand, her other arm wrapped around me. And she's kissing my cheek as I hoist her into the sky.

I bring it with me wherever I go.

"Why?" she whispers. I smile as I shrug.

"Because it's us."

Sixteen Years Ago

EVIE

"I need to finish a few things for work today," my mom says as she walks past my bedroom, "so I will have to meet you there."

I don't say anything.

I just stare at myself in my mirror, my graduation cap on my head, the gown flowing down to my ankles. I have six different tassels for all of my honor societies and extracurriculars. My mom didn't care much about them—she cared more about how much they cost.

When I woke up this morning, I had butterflies. I felt excited. I felt *proud*. I graduated with a perfect GPA. Highest in my class—and that's without the tutors and donations that my classmates' families contributed.

The success I've had was all my own.

I got a full scholarship to NYU.

They have a great social work program.

I am *excited*.

Or at least I was until two minutes ago.

Now, I feel stupid for letting myself feel happy.

Because now, instead of showing up with a gloating family, cameras in hand, tears on cheeks, I'll show up to my own high school graduation alone in a cab. Nan is pretty much wheelchair bound now, and getting her out of her assisted living home is next to impossible. My brother couldn't get off work, so he didn't come into town. I won't know where my family is in the crowd. We won't make plans to go out afterward. My mom won't ask for more pictures of me and my friends.

But I don't cry.

I won't cry.

My makeup is already done.

I've straightened my long locks to all get-out. And there would be no use in being sad. I wish I had a faraway college to look forward to, like my classmates do. They are getting away, gaining independence and new perspectives.

Keaton tried.

He wanted me to go with him to Stanford.

I let him convince me to at least apply. And to my own surprise, I got in. But those loans would have been killer. I would be paying back my education for the rest of my life.

So instead, I'll stay in New York. I'll stay with my mom. I'll commute to my classes, and I'll keep working at the diner.

I'll be smart. I'll be practical.

But sometimes, when I'm alone, I fantasize about going with him, about getting on his dad's jet, flying out west and never looking back, about having my own adventures...and having *him*.

That's what I'm the most scared of.

Keaton has become the most important person in my life over these last four years. And I am absolutely terrified to lose him.

I had my sexual awakening after I watched him run off the lacrosse field last spring. He tugged his helmet off over his head, shaking out his sweaty hair, and I realized then what I'd always been afraid of: I wanted my best friend.

But the problem? So does everybody else.

And the other problem? Everybody else has something else to offer: status, rich parents, a clear, significant place in the world.

Keaton's place has been established since before he was born. His life is predictable in ways that millions of people will never understand.

So I can't want him, because he would be one more thing that I would never get. That I would never deserve. And it might mean that I'd risk losing him altogether. And I don't know that I'd ever recover from that.

Just as I'm about to go downstairs and call a cab, my phone dings on my dresser.

You on your way? he sends. I smile, running my finger over his name.

About to be. Going down to get a cab.

A second barely passes before he's calling me.

"Why are you getting a cab?" he asks.

"She's...gonna be a little late," I say.

There's a beat of silence, and just as I'm about to say that it's fine and I'll see him there, he speaks.

"We will be there in five minutes," he says. "You're not going to our graduation by yourself."

Click.

Sure enough, five minutes later, the Escalade pulls up out in front of our building, and I walk out the front door. I see my mom in our window, watching as I climb in. Her face is expressionless, but I know she's not pleased.

At first, she didn't believe that Keaton and I were friends.

"What on earth would he want with..." she had started to ask once.

But the truth is, I have asked myself that same question a million times. But whatever the reason may be, he's stuck around for four years. While some parents may be thrilled that their child befriended the son of one of the richest men on the planet, my mom used it as another tool in her belt to tear me down. Like there had to be an ulterior motive. Like I didn't offer enough on my own. And unfortunately, her voice has become my inner one.

"You look beautiful, Eve," he says, leaning forward and kissing my cheek. I look behind him as my cheeks flush and see his older brother, Julian, and his younger brother, Brooks.

"Happy graduation day, Evie," Julian says with a nod.

"When can we eat?" Brooks asks, and we both laugh.

GRADUATION GOES OFF WITHOUT A HITCH. I don't hear my mom when my name gets called, but I hear Keaton.

My classmates get loud cheers and whoops and whistles as they walk. Keaton gets a massive round of applause from both his own family and what feels like the entire theater.

His dad gives our closing remarks as the school's largest legacy donor.

And then it's over.

Parents are swarming their kids, camera flashes going off, and I see the not-so-subtle Everett security detail about twenty yards away, creating a large perimeter around them as a ton of the parents gawk at the spectacle.

I sigh.

"*Happy graduation, Keat,*" I whisper to myself. I spin on my heel to attempt to find my mom, when I feel a tap on my shoulder. I spin around to see Russ, one of the family's security guys.

"Keaton wants a picture," he says with a smile. Then he winks. "Happy graduation, Evie."

I smile back.

"Thanks, Russ," I say. He leads me through the crowd, and two of the other bodyguards split apart so we can fit through. Before I can say anything, Keaton rushes me, scooping me up into his arms. He spins me around, hugging me tight.

"Happy graduation day, Evie Rae Dawson," he says, looking up at me as he hoists me up. I smile back.

"Happy graduation, Keat."

He shifts me around so that I'm on his back then nods at his brother.

"Okay, J," he says, "we're ready."

Julian starts snapping pictures as Cato nods and smiles at his onlookers. Brooks is playing on a video game of some sort, and Julian and Keaton's mom, Kitty, is standing next to us, tears in her eyes.

I smile back at her then lean down and leave a kiss on Keaton's face as Julian snaps one more photo. When he sets me back down, he smiles.

"Can you come with us to dinner tonight?" he asks. I tilt my head.

"Keat, I don't want to—"

"I need you there, Eve. Please," he says, his voice just above a whisper. I finally smile and nod. Just like me, he needs a buffer from his own family. And I am happy to be that for him.

A FEW HOURS LATER, I'm combing my hair out and straightening out the long navy dress I chose for dinner when there is a knock on our door.

"Hi, Keaton," my mom answers from the living room, her voice as unenthusiastic as always. I make my way out to where he's standing in our doorway, looking devastatingly handsome in a nice shirt and slacks. *God,* he really is gorgeous. It's sort of unfair to have more wealth than every other human ever and also have gotten the best genes. Leave some for the rest of us. We say a quick goodbye to my mom and make our way down to the car. When we get inside, I gasp.

Nan.

"Nan? What the... How in the..." I start to say as I leap over the seat to wrap her in a hug. She smiles and squeezes me, handing me a card with my name on it.

"It was Keaton's idea," she says. "They came and broke me out on their way here." Tears prick my eyes as I turn to my best friend. He squeezes my knee as I squeeze his hand.

"Thank you, Keat," I manage to say.

A little while later, we are finishing up dinner at some insanely fancy restaurant that I've never even heard of uptown. Cato apparently owns a share of it, and we have the entire place to ourselves. I am so overly stuffed and so uncomfortable.

I'm still not used to being with billionaires, no matter how much I do it. These people have absolutely no concept of the life that most people lead, and we have no concept of theirs. Our realities are different, so when our paths cross, it's just...weird.

But Julian, Keaton, Nan, and I are at one end of the table with Kitty. Cato has some business buddies he's invited at the other end. Brooks is running around the restaurant, and his poor nanny is doing her damndest to keep it together.

Cato finally agreed to let Kitty join for dinner but only after Keaton begged him. Their divorce was so ugly, and I know Julian and Keaton are still not over the way their father treated her. But unfortunately, there isn't much they have the power to do about it—yet.

"Well, I am just so proud of you, Keaty," Kitty says, reaching a hand over to pat his. "You too, Evie. You should be so proud of yourselves."

I haven't spent much time with Kitty, but when I have, I always feel lighter afterward. She's calming, nurturing, empowering.

All the things a mom is supposed to be.

"Thanks, Mom," Keaton says. She smiles then turns back to me again.

"Evie, I just wanted to say thank you."

I swallow.

"Thank me for what?"

"For being such a good friend to Keaton all these years. I hope you two keep in touch. You are good for each other."

"That's the truth," Nan echoes.

Keaton looks at me as he sips his wine that Cato ordered for all of us.

"Yeah," he says. "We are."

Present Day

EVIE

o you need anything before I head out?"
he asks me.

I just shake my head.

"You've done enough," I say, pulling the blanket around me even tighter. But it still falls off one shoulder, exposing my skin, and I swallow. Our eyes meet for a brief moment, and I see him shift. Then he clears his throat.

"Call me if you need anything. And if you don't mind just checking in every once in a while, that would be great. Todd will be here soon. He will be watching the door but can also take you anywhere you want to go."

I force a shy smile and nod.

"You worried about me or something, Everett?"

His face grows more serious.

"Always," he says without hesitation. Our eyes lock, and then I watch as his eyes move over my face. Then he disappears out the door and down the hall.

He kept the picture of us.

It's my favorite one.

I still have a copy of it. It's in a frame, in a box, in the attic of my house.

That I share with my husband.

Shared.

God, I'm a fucking mess.

And if I were anywhere else in the world right now, I am certain that I would be absolutely panicking right now—which, maybe I still will be.

But Keaton makes me feel steady. And just like he always did when were kids, he's the only person who makes me feel like I'm not alone.

I remember when I felt that way about Tanner. Like I was the only person he saw in any room we were in. But then bills got more expensive. Hours at the office got longer. The IVF cost a fucking fortune. And my body *still* couldn't give us a baby.

And then the hormones made the pounds a little slower to fall off. And he stopped looking at me.

And then the drinking got worse.

And worse.

Until I started taking my birth control in secret again. Because I realized that I was scared. *Scared* of my own husband. And I was worried about what bringing a baby into that house might do.

I sit back down on the big couch, wrapping myself up in the blanket I've been living in since he brought me back here last night. It's ultrasoft, and it smells like Keaton. So it's sort of like I'm wrapping myself up in him. And then, I drift off to sleep. Because when I wake up, it's past lunch time. I decide that, today, I'm going to rot in my billionaire best friend's apartment. I order some delivery, and Todd brings it in a little while later.

I grab the remote and turn the TV on, but before I can even scroll, my phone dings next to me. My heart starts racing. I move my eyes to the screen, but I let out a sigh of relief when my mother's name flashes across the screen. She's not my favorite person, but at least it's not Tanner.

"Hi, Mom. How—"

"Did you leave him?" she asks me, a hint of panic in her voice.

I swallow. How the fuck does she know?

"What?"

"Did you leave Tanner last night?"

"Mom, how do you—"

"Yes or no?" she cuts me off again. I swallow back the lump that's forming in my throat. I cry when I'm frustrated, and I can feel it coming.

"Yes," I say simply. I'm not offering her any more.

"Oh, Genevieve," she whispers on the other end, and I close my eyes. "What happened? Where are you?"

I would rather tell her every intimate detail of the downfall of my marriage than give her even the slightest clue as to where I am right now. My parents *loved* telling people that I was friends with an Everett when I was a teenager. So much so that we pretended we drifted apart at one point. I would tell them I was with other friends when I was going to be with Keaton so they wouldn't try to snap a photo or impose. They were grown adults ogling after my friend because of his last name. It always felt so icky. I was so protective of him when we were kids, and judging by the way my body is physically resisting giving any information on him, I guess I still am.

"In the city," I say.

"What happened, Genevieve?"

Ugh. That name.

"He had a lot to drink. We had a big fight. I left," I say.

"Well, are you going back?" she asks. Not, *Are you okay?* or *Do you need anything?* She just wants to know when I'm going back so she's not at risk for having to explain where I am to the rest of the Long Island socialites that she so desperately wants to be a part of.

I feel my blood start to boil inside my veins.

She's never put me first, now included.

"No, Mom. I'm not," I say. I hear a sigh on the other end of the line then a whimper.

"Oh, Genevieve," she says again. "I just...I can't believe this. Are you sure? I mean, can't you—"

"He threw a glass bowl at my feet and held me hostage in my own home. He held my arm so tight that it left a bruise. I'm not going back, Mom. And I'd appreciate some space while I figure out what's next. I'll call when I'm ready," I say, and without another word, I end the call.

And then I feel it. I can't hold them back any longer. And they're not just tears. They are loud, aggressive, visceral sobs. Sobs for the woman who was stuck in that house with that man. Stuck in that *marriage*. Who didn't feel worthy of leaving until right now.

I lower my head down to the couch cushions and let the tears fall, rolling off and soaking into the gray fabric. My phone dings again, and I hold my breath. I almost don't look at it, but it dings again. And when I finally look down, I see it's Keaton.

Todd says it sounds like you're crying? Are you alright?

Todd. That traitor. I sniff and wipe my face, typing back furiously.

I'm all good. You know I've always had a flair for the dramatic.

I send a laughing emoji, but I grow more anxious when he doesn't answer. So I finally put my phone back and lie back down again. I let the tears flow but, this time, quietly. Fuckin' Todd.

But in a few minutes, I jump up when I hear the front door open and shut. I try desperately to wipe the tears from my soaked cheeks, but I'm not fast enough. He walks into the living room, shimmying his coat off and kicking off his shoes. He walks toward me with a brown paper bag and sets it on the coffee table. I stare up at him, but all seeing him does is let the tears come hotter and heavier. He sinks down onto the couch and wraps his arms around me, lying back so that I'm practically on his lap. And then I just let myself cry. I soak his shirt while I cling to the only human who has ever made me feel like my tears mattered.

I cry for the little girl who wanted to change the world but became the woman who smiled even when she was unhappy.

I cry for the girl who thought it would get better when all it got was worse.

I cry for the girl who just wanted the people who were supposed to love her to give a shit.

We're completely horizontal on the couch now, my head on his chest as he strokes my hair. Finally, I feel like I've gotten it all out—at least, for now.

"You hungry?" he whispers when my sobs have subsided. I nod and force out a laugh.

"Crying burns a lot of calories, ya know," I say. He sits us upright, ignoring my quip and reaching for the bag.

"They may be cold, but I grabbed some cinnamon rolls," he says. I look at him and smile. I know I look different than I did when we were kids...than I did when he last saw me. Tanner used to make comments whenever I'd grab something sweet. Keaton is bringing them home to me.

Home.

I really shouldn't be using that term lightly.

This is *not* home. I don't know where home is. But this isn't it.

This isn't even *his* home. This is just a stop on his quest to be back out west.

He walks into the kitchen and pulls down a plate then puts them in the microwave for a few seconds. I follow him in and take a seat at this massive island, and he sets the plate between us.

"Dig in," he says, reaching for one of them and bringing it to his lips. He takes a big, messy bite, and the icing slips off his lips and back onto the plate. I smile as I watch him lick his lips. His lips are pretty.

And based on the zap that just struck, my vagina agrees.

I hesitantly reach in, and he gives me a look.

"You don't want it?" he asks. I shake my head. It smells so good I'm practically

salivating. I just don't want him to know how badly I want to eat it.

"No, I do. I just..."

His eyebrows knit together.

"You just what?"

I smile nervously, tucking my hair behind my ear.

"I probably shouldn't, but—"

"Why not?" he asks. He's just looking at me, his fingers still covered in icing. I swallow.

All of this feels so silly. My entire life has imploded, and I'm worrying about eating a fucking cinnamon roll?

But I guess after years of someone telling you that you shouldn't, you start to believe it.

I lift my eyes to him, and I see something click in

his. His jaw flexes, and his eyes move back forth. Then he looks up at me again.

"Do you want this, Evie?" he asks, his voice low. I bite my bottom lip, then I nod. He reaches his hand out and picks it up off the plate. Then he lifts it to my lips. "Then take it." Our eyes lock, and I lean in, taking a long, painfully slow bite of it. And *God*, it's *good*.

And there is something about the way he's holding it for me, something about the look in his eyes, that sends that zap to my core again.

KEATON

*H*e made her feel like she shouldn't eat.

I'm not sure what went down.

But I know that she was going to stop herself from eating this because there was a voice somewhere inside her telling her she shouldn't.

Motherfucker.

And I know one more thing.

It shouldn't have turned me on so much watching her take that bite. The combination of the white icing on her lips with the look of pleasure on her face... *Fuck.*

We finish eating and clean up, and as I'm putting the plate back, my phone vibrates across the counter. I see Julian's name flashing on the screen, and my heart starts to beat faster. *Fuck.*

I try not to look as anxious as I feel as I swipe it off the counter.

"I gotta take this. I'll be right back," I say, nodding

toward the study. I walk hurriedly down the hall and shut the door behind me.

"J," I breathe into the phone. "What did you find out?"

I hear my brother sigh on the other end.

"It's...it's so much worse than we thought, Keat," he says, just above a whisper.

"How...how much worse?" I ask. I feel my fist clench at my side as I lean back against the desk.

"There are over twenty," he says. "But there could be more. We have only gone back the last ten years. She's going to do some more digging and call me back. We need to meet with legal again tomorrow."

"Yeah, yeah, sounds good," I say. We hang up, and I immediately feel nausea setting in. I put both hands on my desk, trying to let the cool surface bring me back to earth a bit, but it's not working.

My eyes are burning.

The anger is swelling inside of me.

My fucking father.

I always knew he was a piece of shit. But not like this. Not to this many people. Not to women who were just trying to make a goddamn living. I feel the anger building up inside of me, and I swipe the phone off the desk and send it flying across the room. It hits the wall with a *bang*, and I push myself off my desk and walk toward the windows, locking my hands behind my head.

And then I hear the office door creak behind me, making me jump.

"I'm sorry," she whispers. "I just heard a noise and wanted to make sure you were okay."

I don't turn all the way to look at her. I turn back to the window, afraid that I'll fall apart when I see her.

"Sorry about that," I try to say casually. "I'm fine."

But she doesn't leave. Instead, I hear her walking across the hardwood toward me. And then I feel her standing right next to me.

"You can lie to yourself, Keaton," she whispers. "But you can't lie to me."

Fuck. This girl. After all this time, she's right.

Which is exactly why I can't look at her.

She reaches her hand out and grips my sleeve.

"Keat," she whispers, "look at me."

I shake my head slowly, but I feel her move in even closer until our bodies are touching.

Fuck.

She slides her hand down my arm and interlocks our fingers, then she slides her other hand around my arm so that she's hugging it. And I feel the wall I'm desperately holding up start to crumble. Finally, I can't help myself anymore, and I turn and look down at her. Our eyes meet, and I feel myself melt. I start shaking, and her eyes grow wide. She turns me so we're facing each other, and she wraps her arms around me, pulling me in for a long embrace. I hate laying this on her with everything, but the truth is, I need someone right now. I need *her.*

"Talk to me, Keat," she whispers in my ear as she holds me.

I hold back for a moment. This is supposed to stay confidential. It's critical that no one catches wind of any of this.

But it's her.

We may have gone our own ways all those years ago.

But it's still her.

I still trust her with my life.

I slowly nod, pulling apart from her, and lead her to the desk. I sit down at the computer and log into the private, encrypted email account that my brother set up for us while we are working through the case. I draw in a long, slow breath, and then I open up the initial letter.

MR. EVERETT,

ENCLOSED, *please find a detailed statement from a source who says that she was employed by your father during the period listed below and was repeatedly sexually harassed. The source also claims that there are additional victims and that they are also willing to make statements. I would like to meet with you to discuss these claims. Kindly respond by the end of the week. Otherwise, I will have to go to print with the information I have.*

THANK YOU,

. . .

WREN WRIGHT
  Business & News Managing Editor
  Manhattan Times

SHE TURNS TO ME SLOWLY, her hand moving to her mouth.

"Fuck, Keaton," she whispers. "I can't believe this is happening. I'm...I'm so sorry."

I nod.

"Yeah," I say. "It's a clusterfuck. My brothers and I have been meeting with legal to figure out what we need to do—well, brother. Brooks has been scarce, as usual, when the adults are talking. Wren has agreed to give us some time in exchange for us providing whatever we find out."

Her eyebrows knit together.

"Wait...you're *providing* her with information?" she asks. I nod.

"We always knew that Cato was...Cato. But *this...*" I say, standing up from the desk and pacing the room, "he's gone too far. He's hurt too many people. And his 'reign' needs to end now before we lose everything and can't help anyone ever again."

She stands and walks toward me slowly.

"So you're helping to build a case against your dad," she says, putting it all together. I nod. She walks closer to me and takes my hand in hers again. *God*, it feels good when she touches me. "I fucking hate that you have to do this, Keat. But I'm so fucking *proud* of you for it." We look at each other for a moment before she clears her throat and lets her eyes drop. "But I'm so sorry that this has been going on and you've...you've had to deal with me on top of it all. If I had known, I never..."

I scowl and step even closer to her.

"Don't finish that sentence," I growl, cutting her off. "There is *nothing* that should ever stop you from calling me, Evie."

She swallows. I step closer.

"I need to know that you hear me."

"I hear you," she says. But then, I see the look on her face change, and she tilts her

head up to me. "And I need you to hear something too. You always say that I have you. Well, you have me too, Keaton. You always have. I never told you that, and I should have. But I'm telling you now."

I smile down at her. She's cute when she's stern.

"I hear you," I repeat after her. She nods.

"Good," she says. "So, wanna get drunk and talk shit about our fucked-up families?"

I laugh, and it feels good.

"Hell yeah I do."

I grab us some beers from the kitchen, we eat some leftovers, and watch trashy TV. And after a few more beers, she gets up to throw some of the bottles away. As she makes her way back to the living room, she stops and looks down at the giant tablet that controls all the electronics in the room. She gives me a devious look then picks it up. She hits a few buttons, and the lights dim a bit.

She giggles. Then she hits another button. I hear her type something in, then a Beyonce song starts playing, and she starts to sway her hips some. She sets the tablet down, and I lean back into the cushion, just watching.

Fuck, she's beautiful.

And the way her sweatpants are clinging to those hips?

I'm a fucking dead man.

She sways more, lifting her long hair off her shoulders and letting it fall back as she

moves, singing alongto the song as she does. Her eyes are closed, and she looks like a goddamn angel.

A very, very sexy angel.

Her eyes open slowly, and she trains them on me. A shy smile creeps over her lips, and she bites her bottom one. I smile back. Tipsy Evie always got a little more free-spirited, but then she'd catch herself and straighten up.

I don't want her to straighten up right now.

I want her loose, relaxed. Safe.

"You have always loved this song," I say to her, taking a long sip of my beer. She nods.

"Yeah," she says. "This one is my *favorite.*"

"Why is that?" I ask.

"Because it reminds me of you," she says, then she stops moving. She stares at me, eyes wide as saucers, like she can't believe she just said that. If it's possible, she has even more of my attention now. I sit up slightly, taking another sip.

"Why is that?" I ask her. She swallows, biting her bottom lip. Then she shakes her head slowly.

"Nope," she says. "No reason. Pretend I didn't say that."

She starts swaying again, turning her back to me.

But now I need to know.

I scoot off the couch, setting my beer down on the coffee table. As I draw closer to her, it feels like the music is slowing down. It feels like the room is getting a little bit darker, and the only light I see is her. I close the space between us, and she's staring up at me, those long eyelashes batting in my direction. Then she slides her hands up to cover her face.

I reach up and gently move her hands from her face.

"Why does this song make you think of me, Evie?" I ask her again. She takes in a breath.

"Because I had my first orgasm thinking about you while this song was playing," she blurts out. She slaps her hands over her mouth, turning away from me and putting some space between us. So many things are going through my head right now.

The fact that she thought about me in that way all those years ago, when I was across town thinking about her the same.

The fact that I never knew it.

The fact that she *still* thinks about it.

And the fact that she's talking about touching herself to the image of *me*.

My tongue juts out to wet my lip. I close the space between us and reach out to grab her arm. I gently turn her around so she's facing me.

I want to do so many things right now. I want to make her show me. I want to start the song over, pull up a chair, and watch.

I want to help her. With my hands. My mouth. My dick.

I want to watch her come undone for me.

But her face is flushed, she's clammy, and judging by the way she just let that out, she's not in the right state of mind for that. And the first time I make her come, I want her to remember it all. I sigh, bending down to press my forehead to hers.

"Let's go to bed, Eve," I whisper. She just nods against me. I make our bed on the couch, and she's asleep within moments. But me...I'm up and in the shower, trying to let the burning desire I feel for her wash down the drain.

WHEN I WAKE up the next morning, she's gone. And I decide I don't like that as much as when she's here. I grab my phone off the coffee table, and I see that she's texted me.

Had work early today. Repeat of last night later?

I smile as I type back.

Yeah. Complete with the dance. Have a good day at work.

I WONDER how much of last night she remembers. If she knows what she confessed. If she knows how many times I've thought about it since then.

Speaking of work, though, I should probably check in. I do a quick workout in my gym, towel off, and log into my computer while I'm drinking my protein shake. I put out some fires with the non-profit I started, check in with our department heads, and approve some expenses. I check in with my brothers, but there is no news yet.

So I start going a little crazy.

I plop down on the couch again, trying to figure out what to do with myself while she's gone, but all I can think about is how that icing looked on her perfect lips. How warm and soft her hand felt in mine. How I held my breath when she pushed her body up against me last night.

But just as I feel that twitch in my pants, my phone buzzes across the couch. I snatch it up when I see Todd's name on my phone.

"Todd?"

"Sir, he showed up at her office today," he says in one breath, and I feel my own hitch in my breath. "She's okay, a little shaken up. I suggested that she wait in the car until I spoke to you, but she insisted on going inside. I instructed building security not to let him in, but he's still outside."

My jaw ticks as I grit my teeth together. I motion to Mac that we're leaving.

"I'll be there in ten. Text us the address," I say.

I don't even know where her office is.

It could be in Brooklyn or New Jersey for all I know.

But Mac better get us there in ten minutes or less.

Lucky for me, though, it's a nine-minute drive downtown.

And when we pull up, the fucker is still sitting there, leaned against his car. The smug little prick.

The car barely stops before I'm out on the sidewalk, making my way toward him. But before I can put my hands on him, Mac interferes, putting himself between us.

"Are you really this fucking dumb?" I ask him as Mac puts a hand to my chest. "I think I made myself pretty clear the other night."

But Tanner looks a little more with it today than he looked the other night. But the thing about a narcissist is that there is always a way to bring their true self to the surface. You just have to find it. He rolls his eyes but holds his hands up.

"I'm just here to talk to my *wife*," he says sharply, and the word slices through me like a knife.

"Maybe you were too fucked up the other night to remember me telling you that you were not to contact her until she contacted you first."

"Maybe you think because you're rich that people

have to do whatever you say, but this is the real world. And unless you're planning on buying this road and this sidewalk, I'll wait right here."

My fists ball at my sides.

"You—"

"I know who you are, you know," he goes on. And I stand back. This should be good.

"Congrats. You know how to use the internet," I say sarcastically. But to my dismay, he smirks.

"Nah, I talked to her mom," he says. Her fucking mother. If there was ever a time when she should have been there for her daughter, this would have been it. But she failed Evie in this too. "You're Keaton Everett. Her ex-best friend, who she left when she found *me.* Imagine being a fucking *billionaire,* and she *still* doesn't choose you."

I swallow hard.

I see me, on that beach with her, realizing it wasn't going to be me and her.

I see her face, so much pain in her eyes when she told me she couldn't pick me.

I see her face two nights ago, when she needed me.

And I see *red.*

I take a step toward him, but I feel a small hand press between me and him, where she is now trying to intervene.

"Stop!" she says, her little frame wedged between all of us. She looks at me, her eyes boring into mine. "Don't do this. You need to separate yourself from him."

I know she's right.

I know she's talking about the case.

My family can't afford this right now. Just as I'm slowing down my breathing and unclenching my jaw, the idiot speaks up again.

"You know what else is crazy?" he asks with a sadistic smile on his face. "When they say money can't buy everything, well, that's true. Because the only way for her to have a baby is with *me*."

It feels like I've been punched in the stomach. I look at him then at her. She also looks like someone gut-punched her.

"Tanner!" she warns, but it's too late. He can tell he's got her.

"Ah, so she didn't mention that during your little playtime, huh?" he goes on. "They said the eggs they harvested were probably the last viable ones four years ago when we started trying. All she has left are a few frozen embryos. *Our* embryos. Can't buy that, can you?"

My heart is beating so hard that I feel lightheaded. My stomach is turning so much that I feel nauseated.

I walked into this with so much confidence, thinking I could break him. But instead, he broke me.

EVIE

My heart is beating so hard that I feel like I might faint. But I have to keep it together for Keaton. And for me.

I can't believe everything that just happened in the last ninety seconds.

I can't believe that after everything Tanner has put me through, he's still doing it.

Something clicks inside my head.

The disgust I feel toward him. The resentment I have for him. The anger.

It was one thing when he was only hurting me.

But now, he's hurting the most important person in my life, and I just won't have it anymore.

Once I see that Keaton is at a safe enough distance, I turn back to Tanner. Todd is still in my peripheral, so I know I'm okay.

"Maybe it wasn't clear enough when I left the

other night," I say, "but don't contact me again, Tanner."

"Genny—" he starts, but I hold up my hand. Ick. I have always *hated* that nickname.

"Don't come back here. Don't call me. Don't text me."

I turn on my heel, toward the direction where Mac has now escorted Keaton, when I hear him.

"I'll tell you the same thing I told him. You didn't choose him then," Tanner says from behind me. *Fuck.* "You'll remember why soon enough. But don't take too much time. I won't wait around forever."

His audacity stops me dead in my tracks.

"We're all young and dumb at some point, Tanner. And the truth is, I should have chosen *me*. I should have chosen to be alone rather than choose someone who makes me wish I was. And if you think a couple of frozen embryos are enough to put myself through that again, you are more delusional than I ever could have imagined."

I don't even linger to see how big the blow is to his fragile ego. I just hurry along the sidewalk. But I see the black Escalade peeling out.

Keaton.

A FEW MORE HOURS PASS AS I finish up some paperwork for the day. No calls or texts from Keaton, although I do know he's still keeping tabs on me through Todd. I want to get to him. I want to talk to him. Find out how much damage Tanner did. Find out how much hurt he dug back up.

Finally, it's five, and Todd and I are flying out of the office like a bat out of hell.

"Where to?" he asks me when we pull out.

"Just back to the apartment, please," I say.

But when we get back, I'm deflated when I realize he's not here.

I look around, but the apartment is empty. I turn back to Todd.

"Keaton had a dinner event tonight," is all he offers before disappearing back into the study.

A dinner event?

Like, with his brothers?

Like a *date?*

Oh, god. My stomach swirls at the thought of the latter. I nod, walking down the hall to the living room. I order some delivery, flip through the channels, and attempt to read the book I've been putting off for too long.

Finally, I can't wait anymore.

Do you think you'll be home soon? I send off, holding my breath. It's almost eleven, but I can't even think about sleeping right now. Not till I see him. Not till I know if he's okay, or if Tanner just unleashed all the hurt that I caused Keaton all those years ago and never really dealt with.

But before he can answer, I hear the front door

open. I hear him kick off his shoes, and I hear the zipper on his jacket. I swallow and sit up on the couch, turning the volume down. He walks into the room, and my mouth drops open. His hair is slightly out of place, his white button-down highlighting his tan skin, and his eyes as sharp gray as ever. The stubble on his face only accentuates his perfect features. He is fucking devastating in the best way.

"Hey," I say as he walks into the living room. He looks surprised to see me. I swallow, holding my breath, waiting to see if he's sober enough to have this conversation—or any conversation.

"Hey," he says back. "You didn't have to wait up."

"I wanted to," I say. "Unless you don't feel like talking."

He drops his phone and wallet on the table and sits down on the couch. He swipes a hand down his face, and I wait for the smell of alcohol to drift through the air, but it doesn't. All I smell is his panty-dropping cologne.

"We can talk," he says, but he doesn't seem overly enthused.

"Did you...uh, did you have a nice dinner?" I ask. I want him to offer something, anything, to let me know he wasn't with another woman. Imagine that. Me, the married woman shacking up with him because I'm otherwise homeless, jealous that he might have had a date.

"It was fine," is all he gives me. "Did you find something to eat?"

I nod.

"I...I just wanted to talk about what happened with Tanner today," I say nervously. He leans back against the couch. I wait to see if he says anything, but he doesn't. "I...I'm sorry that he—"

"I don't need you to apologize for him."

I swallow.

"O-okay, I just...I guess I just don't know..." my voice trails off. I know there is an elephant in the room. I know we've never talked about it. About the choice I made. About the way I hurt him.

I know I owe him that. I just don't know what to say. Because I was so, so wrong. On so many levels. Even if things with Tanner had worked out, I owed it to the only honest person I had ever known not to abandon him.

"You don't know what, Evie?" he asks, his eyes narrowed on me. His look is so direct, so focused on me that it makes me a little uncomfortable. Like I have a spotlight on me, and he's the only person in the audience.

"I don't know what to say to you," I finally mutter. His eyes stay trained on me. I tuck a lock of hair behind my ear. "I never should have left things the way I did, Keat. I shouldn't have left *you*. And I shouldn't have come crying back to you of all people when the consequences caught up to me. But I did. And I'm so, so sorry. I won't say I regret the choices I made, because I think there is some clarity in all this." I feel the tears stinging my eyes, but I hold them back. He doesn't deserve to have to dry them again. "I just want you to know that you were the most important person in my life then. And it turns out, you still are. I don't want this to feel cheap or like I'm only apologizing now that I'm homeless and on the brink of divorce. But I just needed you to hear it. You are the only person in my life who has been there for me unconditionally. And I know things may be different between us, but I just need you to know how grateful I am to you."

There is a long silence between us, and I can feel my heart thudding in my ears. He stands up slowly, putting his hands in his pockets. Then he finally looks at me.

"And...the uh...the embryos?" he asks quietly without looking at me.

I try to swallow back the tears, but this gets them flowing. I can't not be emotional about this. I'm so... *angry*. I'm so angry about all I went through to *still* not have had a baby. I'm so angry that my marriage is ending the way it is. And I'm so angry that Tanner used my own infertility as a tactic to hurt Keaton without giving me the decency of bringing that up myself.

I move so that I'm sitting on the coffee table in front of him and let out a long, shaky breath.

"That part is true," I say. "We tried for over three years. Nothing stuck, even after all the shots and harvesting and everything else. It took so much out of me. The doctors told us to keep trying, but when we couldn't get pregnant, he started drinking more...so I stopped my treatment without him knowing and started taking my birth control again, just in case." His eyes are locked on me now, and I can't read the expression in them. Something between despair and rage. "There are still a few embryos left," I say, my voice quivering again, "but the truth is...I...I don't know if I could go through all that again. And if I did, it couldn't be with him. I don't want a family with him, Keat. I don't want a future with him." I hold my breath after I speak. Because while I'm confirming that I do not want a future with my husband, I'm also admitting that I don't know if I want to try getting pregnant ever again.

There is a long silence between us for a moment as I try to calm my tears. Finally, he scoots to the end of the couch and reaches a hand out to my face. He swipes my last tear with his thumb, then he puts his other hand on my face and pulls me to him, leaving a long kiss on my forehead. Then he presses his forehead against mine and holds it there for a moment.

"I'm so sorry you went through all that, Eve," he whispers. I open my eyes, but his are closed tight, like he's fighting off some demons. He finally comes apart from me and pushes himself to stand.

"I had dinner with my lawyer tonight," he says. He pulls a business card out of his pocket and drops it on the table in front of me. "If you need him, he will be waiting for your call." There's another pause, and I swallow. He takes a few steps past me then turns around. "You didn't need to apologize to me, Evie. And things between us aren't as different as you think, because if it were up to me, I'd take you to my bed right now and make you forget you were ever his."

I look for a smile or a wink, anything that resembles a joke or an attempt to lighten the mood. But there is nothing. Just a stone-cold expression on his face. And then he turns, walks down the hallway, and shuts his bedroom door behind him.

I lie back on the couch, my mouth still open like a dog salivating for a treat.

Holy fuck.

I swipe the card off the coffee table and twirl it around in my fingers while I walk down the hall to the guest room. I plop down on the cushy bed and look at it.

J.G. Krieger, Esq.

I try thinking about the lawyer. About the severity of the situation. About what going through with a lawyer actually means. New life. New name. New living situation.

But all I can focus on are his words and that pretty mouth that spoke them.

I'd take you to my bed right now and make you forget you were ever his.

I close my eyes and try to picture my life without Tanner.

But instead, all I can picture is Keaton.

Those stormy eyes. That sandy hair out of place from me running my fingers through it. That *body* hanging over top of me.

Fuck.

I toss the card on the nightstand and slide my hand down under my waistband.

I picture his eyes trained on me again. I imagine his scent covering me. And then my eyes roll back.

KEATON

I don't know what finally pushed me over the edge. Maybe it was seeing her rat-faced husband. Maybe it was his words. Maybe it was knowing the dirty details about all that he put her through. Maybe it was her apology. Or maybe a combo of all of it. But I finally had enough of the tiptoeing.

I still want her. I never stopped. I just figured out how to live with it. But now, it feels like I owe it to myself to tell her where I am. To lay it all out. Maybe she will choose the same path she chose before. But at least I know I gave it a shot. I told her where I was. And then I got in the shower and jerked off twice to the thought of it.

STILL NO WORD from my brother today, which means no further update. So I've been in and out of my study, in and out of a few coffee shops, and in the car with Mac for a few hours today, checking in back home and hopping on a few calls.

I saw her this morning before she left for work, but it was a quick good morning and some small talk while she packed her work bag. I haven't heard from her since Todd took her in this morning, and I haven't reached out. I said what I needed to say. If there are any moves left to make, they're hers. I've checked in with Todd to make sure she's safe, but other than that, I'm giving her space.

It's starting to get dark out already when I finally gaze out the window after my last call, and I shut off my computer. But just as I turn my chair toward the door, it opens, and she steps in.

I lean back in my chair as she closes the door behind her. She's dressed in a tight skirt that accentuates her perfect hips, and her heels click across the wood as she makes her way to me. She gets to the other side of my desk and drops a thick folder on my desk. I look at it then up at her.

"What is this?" I ask. She raises her eyebrows and nods toward it. I lean forward and open the top of the folder, and my eyes home in on the words "PETITION FOR DIVORCE" in thick, black letters. I look back up at her.

"I spent the day with J.G. These are being filed this week, and then he will be served," she says. My eyes move back and forth across the words again, as if I don't believe what I'm seeing. Then I lift them to hers. She puts her hands on the desk and leans down over it, giving me a clear shot at her cleavage. I swallow and look back up at her. "Now, make me forget that I was ever his."

I know I should stop this before it gets started. I know I should have done everything I could to not fall back in love with her again.

But instead, I'm running full speed in her direction.

And I'll enjoy every minute of this fiery crash.

I stand up slowly, my eyes trained on her. I walk around the desk slowly, never once taking them off her. I keep walking until we are standing directly in front of one another. We both look a little different than the last time we were together. There's a little more gray in my beard and my hair, a few more wrinkles around both of our eyes. But she's still the most beautiful woman I have ever laid eyes on.

I take one more step so we are chest to chest. I reach my hand up and tuck a lock of hair behind her ear and stroke her jawline with my thumb. I lean down so my lips are next to her ear.

"This can't be undone, Eve," I whisper. I hear her swallow under her breath.

"I'm counting on that," she whispers back, and I can't help but smile.

"We won't ever go back to what we were. Or what we are now. Nothing will be the same," I tell her. But she just nods, and I think maybe I'm also telling myself. But the truth is, after she left the first time, nothing ever was the same.

She was the sun that my world revolved around, and when she left, my world went dark. And the crazy thing is that, even after everything, after a part of me died, I know that one look from her would have lit up my entire soul again. And I know that because, two nights ago, when I walked into that diner, that's exactly what happened. She breathed life back into me with one look. If she never came back again after this, I would live the rest of my life in a purgatory of my own design, because being apart from her wouldn't really be living in the first place.

I cup her head in my hand, staring down into those same eyes that made my body react all those years ago.

"Fuck it," I say, and my lips crash onto hers. A little whimper escapes her, and it makes my whole body vibrate. I hold her head between my hands, savoring her lips against mine. I start slowly, kissing her for sixteen-year-old Keaton, who wants nothing more than to make her feel like the most special girl in the world. Then I kiss her harder, more urgently. This time for twenty-one-year-old Keaton, who is terrified she's going to slip out of my grasp. Then my tongue slips between her lips, claiming her for thirty-four-year-old Keaton, who has waited long enough, and who isn't going to let her go again.

I slip my arms around her, scooping her up and walking out of the study. She tightens her arms around my neck, one hand curling around it and one weaving through my hair. I slide my hand up her back, the other hooked under her legs as I nudge my bedroom door open then kick it shut with a thud.

God, it feels so fucking good to kiss her. After all this fucking time, to have her to myself. Even if it's just for tonight. But God, I hope it's not.

I kick my shoes off as I walk across the room, making my way toward the bed. I lay her down slowly, my head under her hand, our lips never coming apart. I run my hands down her body, over her hips, and around to her ass. The perfect fucking handful.

My Evie.

She fits so perfectly with me.

She moans as I give her a little squeeze, and I smile against her mouth. I move my hands toward the waistband of her leggings, slipping my fingers in. She bucks against my touch, her fingers weaving through my hair. I tug on the leggings, and her eyes open. We come apart as I look down at her, making sure she's okay with the direction this is going. She doesn't say anything but just nods.

I tug them down slowly, and as I do, I realize she has no underwear underneath them.

Fuck. Me. My eyes flick up to hers, and she bites her lip nervously. I pull them down farther, until she's completely exposed to me, and I salivate at the sight of her. After all this time, after everything we have learned about each other, all the secrets we know, there are still parts that we've kept from one another.

And that changes tonight.

I stare down at her perfect pussy, then I look up at

her and lick my lips. I pull the leggings all the way down and tug them off her feet. I run my hands up her legs, leaving soft kisses on the insides of her calves and up her thighs. When I push her legs apart, she jolts, and I lock eyes with her.

"Do you want me to stop, Eve?"

She bites her lip then shakes her head slowly.

"No, I just don't want you to feel like you have to," she says shyly. I lift an eyebrow. She lets out a little shuddered breath. "I can...I can take a while. And I don't want it to get old. Plus, I...I haven't shaved and—"

"How about this, baby," I cut her off. "How about you just lie back and let me go. If you don't like it, you just tap my arm, and I'll stop. Okay?"

She bites her lip again. Then she nods slowly.

I move to push her legs apart, but they're stiff. I squeeze them gently, leaning down so that my mouth is just inches from her pussy.

"Relax, baby," I whisper. "I've been wanting to do this for twenty years." Her eyes open wide as she lets her head sink back in the mattress, but her legs flop to the sides, and I smile. And then I dive in. I start off slow with long swipes of my tongue. And holy *fuck* does she taste good. I feel another shudder go through her, and I moan.

"Jesus," I say, and her eyes shoot open again. "You taste amazing, Eve." I see her visibly relax a little more, and I get back to work. My tongue works her folds, and I suck her into my mouth, playing with her, licking and flicking her clit with my tongue. She starts to writhe under me, and I can tell it's working. And all it does is make me want to keep going.

I don't want it to get old.

Ha. If that fucker ever made her feel that way, he can go fuck himself.

Literally. Because after tonight, there's no way he's ever fucking her again.

When she starts breathing more erratically, I slip a finger inside her. Her hips buck against my mouth, and she lets out a soft moan that makes me as hard as a fucking brick. Then I slip another in, hooking them around until I find the spot that makes her slam her hands down on the bed. She's pressing herself up into me and pushing her head farther down into the mattress.

Then she starts gasping for air. I reach my other hand up and press down on her stomach, moving my tongue and fingers in the same rhythm until I feel her body start to shake. She fists a clump of my hair and sucks her teeth, and I smile as I devour her.

I feel her start to tense up again, and I push my fingers in deeper.

"Stop thinking, sweet girl," I tell her. "Stop thinking and just feel me."

Her legs flop out again, and she loosens her grip on my hair while I dive back in. I suck her clit into my mouth and curve my fingers upward, pumping them in and out until I feel her legs stiffen around me.

She gasps and moans, and then her free hand

slides up and under her shirt. She lifts it up, exposing her perfect breast, and tugs on her nipple, and then I think *I* might come. But I have a job to finish.

I massage her with my tongue for another moment, and then she screams out my name while her body vibrates beneath me.

I give her one more lick before I slide back and pull my fingers from her.

She's panting with one arm draped over her eyes. Her legs are still flopped to the sides, and one breast hangs out of her shirt. I smile as I leave a trail of kisses back down her legs then reach up to tug her shirt off over her head.

I look down at her perfect body, different from the one I used to know, but my absolute favorite version of her. Her pink nipples are pointed toward the ceiling, leading down to the perfect curves of her hips, her pussy still glistening.

"You are the most beautiful woman in the entire fucking world, Evie Rae Dawson," I tell her. She finally opens her eyes, her breathing calming down, and she smiles at me. But then she becomes aware of the fact that my eyes are scouring her body, and she folds her leg over the other and drapes an arm over her chest and mid-section.

I wince.

Watching her hide herself, watching the nerves she has when she realizes my eyes are on her...it feels like shame. And it makes me sick.

"Thank you for that," she says, motioning toward

my mouth as her grip around herself tightens a little more. "You didn't have to do that."

"Did you not like it?" I ask her. She scoffs.

"Of course I did," she says. "I've never, um... That's never... I've never felt that before." I reach down and tug my shirt off over my head. Now her eyes are the ones scouring. She sits up, reaching for my zipper with her free hand. But her other arm still covers her midsection. I stop her hand, and she looks up at me. "It's your turn," she says.

I reach down and take her other hand off her stomach gently. I bring it to my lips without breaking eye contact with her, and I kiss her palm.

"This isn't a tit-for-tat game, sweet girl," I tell her. "Sometimes, it's going to be all about you. I am going to worship every single inch of this body of yours. Now, stop hiding yourself from me, Eve. I've waited too long to have you, and you have never been more beautiful than you are right now."

She swallows, and I realize her eyes are getting glassy. Her hand slips out of my grip and goes to her stomach again. She rolls her lips, and I lean forward. I put my lips on her stomach, kissing it and pushing her back gently. Then I lift my eyes to hers.

"Every. Single. Inch," I tell her, and then I push my jeans and boxers down. I spring free, and her eyes open like saucers. Her tongue juts out to lick her lips, and then she looks back up at me. She props herself up on her elbows and bites her bottom lip.

"You good?" I ask her with a smile. She nods, her eyes moving between mine and my cock.

"Mm-hmm," she says. "I just...I always wondered if I was right about you. Turns out, I am."

"Right about what?"

"About you having a huge dick," she says matter-of-factly. I throw my head back and laugh, but I jolt when I feel her hand wrap around me. She pumps it up and down, and our eyes lock.

"What did I tell you?" I ask her, trying to keep my cool while trying not to bust in her hand. Her eyes move up to me as she moves her mouth closer to my shaft.

"Sometimes it's going to be all about me," she says, "which is fine. Because right now, all I want is your cock in my mouth."

Holy fuck.

EVIE

I hated giving Tanner head.

Hated it.

I hated the way he tasted. I hated the way he forced my head down. I hated the way he asked for it multiple times a week.

But right now?

I've never been so desperate to wrap my lips around a penis in my life.

He gives me a look, but I ignore it. I stick my tongue out and trace his shaft, and he hisses.

"Eve..." he starts to say, but before he can get it out, I'm on my knees in front of him, taking him into my mouth. I put my hands on his hips, holding myself steady as my head bobs back and forth. "Oh, my sweet girl," he whispers as I move. I moan underneath him, and he strokes my hair gently. "You're doing such a good job, baby." I relish in his praise, cupping his balls in one hand and clawing his thigh with the other. I move back and forth, moaning and groaning as I take him in as deep as I can. I jerk back when he steps away, but before I can ask him what the deal is, he's hooking his hands underneath my armpits and lifting me off the ground.

"You're amazing at that, Evie," he says. "And as much as I'd love to come in your mouth, I'm coming inside of you tonight."

I swallow and wipe the corners of my mouth.

"If that's okay with you," he says. I smirk as I lean back on the bed, spreading my legs for him. I don't know what switch he just hit, but I feel so much bolder than I've felt in my entire adult life right now.

"I think that could work," I say, tugging on one of my nipples again as I bite my bottom lip. He smirks and reaches for his nightstand drawer. "What are you doing?"

He pauses.

"I was gonna grab a condom," he says.

I feel a wave of disappointment.

"I appreciate that," I say, "and if you want to use one, I totally understand. But the only person I've been with in the last decade is Tanner. And I'd really love to feel you...*all* of you."

He stares down at me, and his hand slowly closes the drawer. He takes a step toward me, then another, and puts his hands down on either side of me, leaning in so our faces are just inches apart.

"I was just trying to be respectful," he says. "But

the image of me dripping out of you is one I'd love to see come to life."

I swallow.

Jesus, me too.

"But baby?" he says.

"Hmm?"

"That's the last time we are ever going to talk about him fucking you," he says, then he yanks me down toward the edge of the bed. He spits in his hand and pumps it up and down his cock, then he spits on my pussy and rubs me gently before priming me with a finger. Then, when he knows I'm ready, he pushes himself into me, and I cry out.

"Jesus," I moan as he stands up straighter, aligning our hips and holding me in place. He moves his hips slowly back and forth, allowing me to adjust to him. Then he starts to move faster.

And I enjoy it.

I enjoy it *loudly*.

Sex has never made me make noises before. They were mostly for show. They were mostly to help Tanner feel like he was actually doing something to me. To get him off quicker so I could roll back over and pretend it didn't happen.

But tonight? He's touching me in places I didn't know existed. He's holding my body in positions like he knows what's best for it. And the thing is, he *does*. He moves faster and deeper at the same time, all while watching my face to gauge what's working. But right now, it feels like it all is.

His ab muscles flex into the most delicious fucking V I've ever seen just above his cock, which, by the way, is the most beautiful penis I've ever seen. There's a shimmer of sweat on his chest beneath speckles of brown curls, and I want to lick it off.

I stare at him while he pounds into me, pretty positive that there isn't a single inch of his body I wouldn't put into my mouth.

"Do you know how long I have wanted this, Evie?" he groans. I can't respond with words. Instead, I just push my head back into the mattress and claw at his shoulder. "So fucking long. You were supposed to be mine all along, honey. All. Along," he says, pounding into me in rhythm with his words.

I'm panting, but I reach a hand up to his face.

"I'm sorry," I moan out. "I'm so fucking sorry."

There is something so erotic in his confession and even in my apology. It's like our first time and make-up sex all combined into one beautiful night. He freezes above me for a moment, and the blood drains from my face when I realize that the bliss between my legs is on pause.

"Don't apologize to me, Evie," he says sternly. "Just say you're mine."

Our eyes lock, and I realize he's being serious. Totally, completely serious. He needs to know.

I push myself up onto my elbows and reach one hand up to wrap around the back of his head.

"I have always been yours," I tell him. "Even when I was his." Then I pull him down into me, our lips and tongues crashing together. He lets go of my hips to hold my head to his, like this kiss is his lifeline. When we finally come apart, I have a newfound bolt of confidence...and an insatiable hunger for him. I put one hand on his chest and scoot toward the end of the bed. "Let me show you how sorry I am."

I stand up, grabbing his arm and swinging him around so that he's now on the bed. I push him down then crawl up his body, pausing ever so quickly so that my breasts dangle in his face for a moment. A devilish smile creeps over his lips as I straddle him then lower myself down onto him without taking my hands off his chest. He moans with pleasure as I bite my lip.

I move my hips back and forth, letting him fill me up from below, my hands still splayed out on his chest. And then I lift my ass up and down, sliding up and down his dick while I dig my fingernails into his shoulders.

"Fuck, Keat," I moan out. "I can't believe I waited this long."

He smiles beneath me, reaching up to palm my breasts as I bounce higher and higher. I feel him in my stomach, and it's the most intense pleasure I've ever had.

"Yeah?" he breathes. "You like it?" I nod, like an addict who has her eye on the prize. He sits up, his hand sliding up my back, then carefully and methodically, he slides out of me and flips me onto my stomach in one quick, pretty move. He pulls me up in front of him so that we are back to chest, one hand wrapping gently around my neck and the other sliding down between my breasts, over my navel, and to my pussy. His fingers glide through my arousal, keeping me nice and wet. My whole body is practically purring for him.

"I have a whole lot of making up to do, sweet girl," he whispers in my ear, leaving a soft trail of kisses and chills up my spine. "And I'm not stopping till I claim every single inch of you. Buckle up, baby girl. You're mine now."

"Mmm," I moan, practically melting into him. "Yours," I echo him. And with that, he pushes into me from behind then fucks me like he's afraid I'm going to disappear. He holds tight to my hip, one hand wrapped around my hair, and we move back and forth together, me matching his every motion. "Good, baby. You're doing so great. You can take it, Eve."

His praise is all I need to throw myself back into him, over and over, matching his thrusts. I claw for the covers, and his hand slides down to my clit. He rubs it in the most perfect circular motion, pressing into it just the right amount and at just the right time with each motion. And then I feel my legs start to tingle. And my toes. And I moan—no, not moan...*scream*—out his name. He fucks me even harder until I hear his growl, and he collapses on top of me. After a few moments of catching our breath, he slides out of me slowly, and I fall forward onto the bed. I feel the wetness slide out of me and drip down my leg, and then I feel the swipe of his finger.

"There it is," he growls into my ear. "*Mine.*"

KEATON

I've wondered what it would be like to sleep with Evie Dawson for two decades.

I wanted her so badly when we were young.

I wanted her for my own selfish needs and desires.

But now, tonight, I wanted her for *her* too. I wanted her to know what it felt like to be worshipped. For someone to absolutely, desperately need her. Because I sure as hell did. And even now, seeing myself sliding down her thigh, I *still* do.

She looks so fucking beautiful lying here on my bed, naked, slick with both of our sweat. Her hair is splayed out over my pillows like flames, one arm draped up over her head while the other is draped subtly over her mid-section.

I hate that she feels like she has to cover up.

Especially now.

I'm about to walk to the bathroom to get her a towel, but I stop and lean over her on the bed. I lean down so our lips are just centimeters apart, and I slowly take her hand from her stomach and bring it to my lips.

"Stop. Hiding," I tell her, kissing her hand twice. She smiles, her cheeks flushing, and she turns to her side, this time with her hands both tucked under her head. I smile and walk to the bathroom. After I clean us both up, I hit the switch on the remote that's attached to the wall. The blinds lift, and suddenly, we are looking out over Manhattan. It's a clear night, and it feels like you can see the whole island.

"Show-off," she says with a playful smirk, and I gently tap her ass as I climb into the bed next to her. I hit another button on the remote next to me, and the gas fireplace in the corner of the room turns on. I look over at her.

"You ain't seen nothin' yet," I say playfully as I tickle her sides. She shrieks as I pull her into me, nuzzling into her hair and neck. She wraps her arms over mine tightly, and we just lie here under the glow of a fake fire and the New York skyline.

We lie in silence for what feels like only a few moments but ends up being a solid hour before she finally turns to me. I know she has something on her mind by the way she keeps rolling her lips together. Her eyes move from point to point on my face. I smile and tuck a stray lock of her hair behind her ear.

"What is it?" I whisper. Her eyes lock on mine, and she smiles, knowing she's been caught in the act of overthinking.

"What now?" she whispers back. "What does this mean?"

I smile back at her while I watch the thoughts run through her brain, like a hamster on a wheel. Never stopping. Never slowing down. New ones growing off the others like branches. And never slowing down to let her see what's in front of her.

"Well, honey, that's really up to you," I tell her honestly. "You're the one with the decisions to make here. But for me, it's really only ever been you. And it still is. I can tell you one thing, though...that if you let me, I'm going to spoil the fuck out of you." She giggles, and I smile, but I'm serious. "I mean it, sweet girl. You are so turned around from these years of never being first that you don't even know what it looks like. Even with your folks, your brothers...no one has ever put you first. You've never seen it done. But if you're ready, that stops now. And if you're not, then it will stop whenever you are." She blinks rapidly as she stares back at me, and I see the tears pooling in her eyes. "No, baby, no. No tears," I tell her. She smiles as she blinks them back, but one slips from the corner of her eye, and I swipe it away with my finger.

"It should have been you, Keat," she whispers, her lip trembling slightly. I lean forward and kiss her lips softly.

"We ain't dead yet, sweet girl. There is still plenty of time."

We go for round two—this time a much sweeter, more innocent version. I help her come first, and then I come while I look down into her eyes. And then we fall asleep, naked and wrapped up in each other. I swear I could die a happy man if my story ended right here.

WHEN I WAKE up the next morning, I hear the shower running. I blink a few times, clearing the haze from my eyes. It's a cloudy day in New York, and mornings like these make me miss this place that I used to call home. I love New York when it's gloomy like this. I slip out from the covers and make my way to the bathroom. I pause at the doorway, watching her wash her hair in my extra-large shower, humming some song I can't place while she moves. I could stare at her like this forever, but instead, I pad across the cool tile floor and open the shower door, stepping in behind her. She doesn't turn around. She just reaches for me with her free hand and pulls me under the water.

"Good morning," she hums, and I smile and kiss the side of her neck.

"Good morning, beautiful," I say, reaching for the soap and one of the extra-expensive loofahs that the family interior designer demanded I have here. I thought it was silly then. But now, as I lather it up and rub it gently across her bare back, I'm pretty happy I went along with it. "Why are you up so early?" I ask her.

"I want to go into the office to finish up some paperwork today," she says. "I have been swamped and a little distracted." She gives me a little look that makes me want to devour her. I nuzzle into her neck.

"Sorry, not sorry," I tell her. She giggles and spins around to me, throwing her arms up around my neck.

"Keat," she says, her tongue jutting out to wet her lips.

"Hmm?" I ask, feeling myself growing harder by the second. Watching the water droplets make their way down to her nipples has me salivating.

"I want you to feel worshipped too," she says, leaning forward to place a kiss on my pec. "Not because you're an Everett," she says, kissing the other one, "but because you're *you.*"

"Oh yeah?" I ask her, feeling my throbbing cock press against her as she steps closer.

"Yeah," she whispers in my ear as she kisses the side of my neck.

"How do you plan on doing that?" I ask her. She looks up at me, her eyes hooded, and bites her bottom lip. Then she slinks down to her knees, and I brace myself against the wall.

She grabs my thigh with one hand and uses the other to pump my cock up and down until I'm standing straight up. Then she looks up at me one more time with those big, eager eyes and takes me into her mouth with one big gulp.

My breath hitches in my throat as I drop my head back for a moment, reeling in the sensation of her warm mouth wrapped around me. But I want to see it. I want to watch Evie Dawson taking me into her mouth like she's ravenous. So I do. I look down and see her looking up at me, those big green eyes opened wide and watering as I get dangerously close to the back of her throat.

"Oh, honey," I spit out as she moves her mouth farther down my shaft. I feel her swallow back, and that sensation almost puts me over the edge. I tap the sides of her arms lightly, and she slows down. "Come up, baby."

She looks up at me, confused.

"I'm about to blow, baby."

But she doesn't stop. She grips me tighter, moving her head faster, sucking me harder, and making me see fucking stars. I brace myself again, one hand against the shower wall, the other wrapped in her soaking-wet hair. I feel it starting at my base, pulsating up my cock. And then I come in her mouth.

I wait for her to hop off, but she doesn't. She just keeps moving until I moan, my legs feeling like they're going to buckle beneath me. She waits until my noises stop, till she knows she's gotten all there is to get out of me. She slowly slides off me, and I watch her swallow it all down.

Fuck. Me.

She wipes the corners of her mouth then stands up, letting the water run over her. I step toward her once I've gotten my bearings, my hand sliding up between her legs. But she catches me.

"Ah-ah," she says with a smile, "sometimes it's about you."

Then she spins on her heel and gets out of the shower.

TWENTY MINUTES LATER, she's dressed in a pencil skirt and a white blouse, her hair tied up in a tight bun, looking all professional and not at all like the girl who was just on her knees for me a few minutes ago.

I watch her step into her heels, savoring every curve of her body, before walking over and pulling her into me for a long kiss.

"I don't like when you leave," I tell her. She smiles against my mouth.

"Ditto," she says. "I won't be too long. Just want to finish up a few things before the weekend."

I nod, kissing her one more time.

"I'll be here on some calls this morning," I tell her. "I already can't wait to see you."

She smiles as she blows me one more kiss before she and Todd get on the elevator.

I SPEND the next few hours on some calls, responding to about eight hundred and seven emails, and getting my third cup of coffee. I'm really excited about some projects that we are kicking off in California. A self-sufficient farm that will run by labor of un-housed citizens in the downtown LA area. We plan to build temporary housing for them on the property so they have somewhere to live while they work.

Another project is an organization that will help connect victims of domestic violence with affordable housing, career coaching, and therapy.

They are small initiatives in a small corner of the country. But my grandfather always told us: "Goodness spreads. Plant the seed, and watch it grow."

So that's what I'm doing.

I know my brothers are too—well, at least Julian. He is hiding under the guise of being in charge of Everett Enterprises alongside our father, but he's using that as a cover. He's been utilizing Everett resources for years, trying to make his own small changes within the enterprise and outside of it.

We've been combatting our father's greed for our whole lives.

But now we have to do it bigger—and do it faster.

I'm about to get dressed to go for a run when I see my brother's name flash across my screen.

"Hey, J," I say.

"Hey," he huffs back. "She wants to meet. Can you come tonight?"

I swallow, my heartbeat thudding in my ears. I feel my stomach start to churn.

"Yes, of course," I say as my office door nudges open.

And then I see her.

And I instantly feel calmer.

"Eight o'clock," he says.

"See you then," I say, pressing end.

She just stares at me, her bag still on her shoulder and her shoes still on.

"I want to come with you," she says. My eyes widen.

"My brothers will be there," I tell her. She knows what it means. They know her. Julian, especially, knows what happened between us. He knew how I felt about her. He knew she left. He knew I was crushed, because he spent six months flying out to California every few weeks to check in on me.

We won't be able to hide it.

They'll know.

"I know," she says. I walk around the desk toward her.

"So, are you..."

"I don't care," she says. "I want to be there for you." I reach out and take her hands.

"I love that," I say, "but if you're not ready—"

"I'm ready, Keat," she says. "I've always been ready for us. I just didn't think I deserved it."

I smile as I lean down to kiss her. But she steps backward. I give her a confused look, but her eyes stay trained on mine. She pushes me back down into my chair, wheeling me back slightly. Then she hops up on my desk.

She crosses her legs first then slowly pulls the top one down.

She spreads them slowly, her pencil skirt riding up her thighs.

My cock stiffens in my pants. She lifts one heeled

foot up and puts it on one of my armrests, her eyes never leaving mine.

"Eve," I whisper, but she just puts a finger to her lips. Slowly, she lifts the other foot, and her skirt lifts even farther. And then I realize that she has nothing on underneath it.

"Do you want to know something, Keaton Everett?" she asks. I clear my throat and nod, but I can't take my eyes off her perfect pussy.

My pussy.

"I have been picturing you while I get myself off for over two decades," she says, then she leans back on her elbows.

Fuck. Me.

"Is that so?" I say, trying to keep my voice calm and even.

She nods, bringing the pads of her fingers to her lips. Then she sticks her tongue out and wets them.

I'm going to fucking bust in my pants.

She slides her hand down her body painfully slow.

"I just slide my fingers down like this," she says, moving her fingers to her opening, "and start to picture you. Your body. Your eyes. Your hands...everything," she says between moans. She starts to pick up the pace, and I scoot forward. But she uses one heel and presses it against my chest, keeping me in the chair.

I am fucking dying.

Her hand moves quicker, and her other hand slides up to palm one of her breasts through her shirt.

"I'd picture you doing all kinds of things to me," she moans and bites her lip. "But now...oh...now? Now I'm going to picture that huge fucking cock filling me up. Every. Single. Time."

She rubs faster, harder, alternating between pressing her clit and fingering herself.

I am salivating. I am sweating. I am *dying* to touch her. Taste her. *Anything* she will give me. But she just presses her foot against me harder.

"I think about your smile, your voice...oh," she whines, "and now, I'll think about the way you were so, so deep inside of me. So fucking deep."

"Fuck, Evie," I groan. "Please."

She opens her eyes as she rubs herself harder, licking her lips.

"You want to help?" she asks, and I nod like an idiot. She waits a beat, pressing harder and faster. Then finally, she moves her foot, letting me pass. I dive in, offering her my mouth while her hand keeps working. I suck her folds into my mouth, letting my tongue slide in and out of her while her fingers still work on her clit. And then she's close, her head dropping back, and I take over. I plunge two fingers deep inside of her, hooking them around while I lick. She lets out the most delicious growl as she clutches my hair, then her body goes limp on my desk. We are both sweating and panting, and I gently tug her skirt back down over her thighs. I help her sit up, then I lean in.

"You deserve the fucking world, Eve," I whisper, "and I'm going to give it to you."

EVIE

I never knew that my sex life could be so good I'd need a nap to recover.

But here I am.

A few hours later, I'm in Keaton's bathroom, tugging my hair up into a bun. I couldn't decide what sort of outfit says, *Sorry your dad sucks, sorry I broke your brother's heart, and also, I'm back.* So, I settled on jeans and my favorite green-and-black flannel.

I slip on my old white Nikes and walk out of the primary suite, padding down the hall toward the living room. As I do, I stop for a moment when I catch a glimpse of myself in the hallway mirror.

I look like I'm comfortable here.

Like I know my way around.

Like I'm home.

I don't know if that's right or not. All I know is, I feel grounded when I'm wherever he is.

When I step into the living room, he's on the

phone. The expression on his face looks serious, but it lightens when he sees me. I make my way across the room to him, and he holds an arm out for me. I nestle into him as he ends his call, and he leans down to leave a kiss on my temple.

"Ready?" I ask him. He sighs and presses his head to mine.

"No. But let's go anyway."

Five minutes later, we're in the back of the black Escalade on our way to Julian's. The ride over is quiet. He's staring out at the city, and I'm staring at him. I'm trying to channel my own anxiety about seeing Julian again into the need to be there for Keaton. The need to make him the center of everything tonight. Put all my energy in him.

But as Mac turns the car into the driveway of a garage under a very tall building and scans a badge, I feel my nerves begin to dance.

I haven't seen Julian Everett since I was twenty years old. Julian is a hard read on a good day, but he always looked out for Keaton. Keaton was arguably the most important person in Julian's life when we were younger. And then Brooks too, when he came along. Julian tried to protect them from the insanity that was and is their family. He followed the exact schooling and career path that their father wanted so that when it was Keaton's turn, it wasn't such a big deal.

I remember Keaton telling me one time that the night their mom died, he couldn't stop crying. Julian came in his room, sat on his bed, and held him like he was a small child.

Keaton has always danced to the beat of his own drum, but he didn't escape the guilt that came from leaving his big brother to take all the responsibility and scrutiny.

Brooks is a different story. He is eleven years younger than Julian and eight years younger than Keaton. He has a different mom than the older two and had a much different life. I knew him as the spoiled rotten kid who had the most fucked-up, warped sense of reality. Based on the clips I've seen on social media, he has now turned into a grown-up with a fucked-up, warped sense of reality.

When I last saw Brooks, he was a bratty twelve-year-old kid. He doesn't intimidate me.

But Julian is a different story. He was there for Keaton's and my story. He doesn't trust people. And to be fair, I'm not sure I deserve his trust.

When Mac puts the car in park, Keaton gets out and holds out his hand for me.

"Let's do this," he sighs as we walk through the door and get into the elevator. Mac scans a badge again then presses the button that says *penthouse*. We ride in silence, and I rub my thumb over the back of his hand until the doors ding.

And then I'm in awe. I've never been to this apartment before. Julian didn't live here when Keaton left town. It feels...big. Keaton's apartment is fit for someone very, very rich. But it's not a penthouse in downtown Manhattan. It's more modest. It feels less lived-in. Less customized.

Julian's apartment is fit for a king. Not *a* king. More like king of the fucking universe. It's massive. Cathedral ceilings in a fucking *apartment.* Floor-to-ceiling windows everywhere you look, like I'm watching Manhattan on an IMAX screen.

It's impeccably decorated, a large painting of Kitty hanging on one wall. It's sleek, modern, and completely spotless, and I immediately feel even more anxious. I expect it to be busy with help, maids, chefs... but instead, there is no one except for Mac and another man who looks like he's security too.

I swallow when, around the corner, pads in a petite little brunette with a big smile on her face. She can't be more than twenty-one or twenty-two years old. Then I remember seeing this online too.

"Hi, Keat," she says, arms outstretched. She takes him in for a hug and rubs his back as her eyes land on me. "Who is—"

"What's going on?" a booming voice from the back of the room commands. Julian looks the same. Maybe a few more wrinkles around his eyes but, otherwise, the same. His eyes bounce from me, to Keaton, back to me, back to Keaton. "Evie?" he asks. I relish in the way he says my name. Other than Keaton, he's the only other person who has ever called me Evie that first knew me as Genevieve. Once he found out I preferred it, he never wavered.

He may not have liked me, but he respected me.

"Hi, Julian," I say sheepishly. Keaton gives my hand a knowing squeeze. "It is really, really good to see you."

His eyebrows knit together as he comes closer, placing his hand on the brunette's back. She looks at him, then to me, then thrusts her hand out.

"Since Julian is being rude, hi," she says with a smile. "I'm Sawyer."

I take her hand and smile back.

"I'm Evie," I say. There's a long silence, like everyone is waiting for me to provide some context. But I don't know what context to give them. *I'm Keaton's ex-best friend, who desperately called him a few days ago and has since then filed for divorce and fucked him repeatedly,* just doesn't feel like it's going to be the smoothest.

"Evie was Keaton's best friend growing up," Julian says for us as he looks back and forth between us again. "And now she's...back?"

Keaton smiles, bringing my hand to his lips.

"She's back," is all he offers his big brother, and that seems to be enough to suffice. Maybe it's the distraction of everything with Cato, or maybe it's this new girl who's softened him up a bit. But either way, I let out a sigh of relief as he gives me a nod then leads us into his study.

There is a large wooden table in the corner of the room by the windows, and he leads us to it and motions for us to sit down.

He lifts up a folder then looks at Keaton.

"I assume that..." Julian says, motioning to me. Keaton nods.

"She knows," he says. Julian nods slowly.

"I would never—" I start to say, but Julian just nods.

"I know," he says. "I know. And I wish we had some more time for you two to catch me up on what the hell is happening with you two right now, but the reporter will be here any minute, and she has requested that she just meet with us brothers—at least for this first time. Of course, Brooks bailed again. And I'm not waiting on his ass. Are you two okay waiting upstairs?" Julian looks at Sawyer and me.

I look at Keaton. He gives me a sad smile and nods.

"I will do whatever you guys need me to do," I say.

"We will go hang upstairs," Sawyer says. "Let us know if you need us. Come on, Evie. We'll get some grub and watch shitty TV."

I smile.

"Sounds great." I turn back to Keaton, eyeing the folder. I put my hand on his face. "I'm right here."

He leans forward and kisses my cheek again.

"I know."

With that, I follow Sawyer out of the study, down the hall, and up the massive floating staircase.

"This place is nuts," I say as I look out over the city. She giggles.

"I thought I'd be used to it by now, but I don't know if I ever will be," she says. We walk into what looks to be a large rec room with a red-velvet pool table in one corner, an air hockey table at the other, three huge couches, some arcade games, and a TV screen that is the size of the entire wall. There is also a full stocked bar, a coffee bar, and what appears to be a vending machine.

She walks to the bar and goes behind it, grabbing two glasses.

"Want anything?" she asks.

I think about it. A nice glass of whiskey sounds good right now to calm my nerves, but I want to be in the right headspace for him. I want to be ready when he's done and needs me.

"Maybe just a seltzer water?" I ask. She nods, and I see that she's making herself a sweet iced tea. She comes around and hands me the glass then leads me toward the couches. We plop down, and she leans over to hit a few buttons on a remote that looks more like a tablet. The lighting above us dims a bit, and the massive television turns on. The channel switches to a trashy dating show, which is exactly what I'd be putting on if I were alone, stressing right now. Then she turns to me.

"So," she says, pulling her legs up underneath her, "since we didn't really get an intro earlier, want to give me yours?"

I smile, turning to face her and pulling my legs up too.

"What do you want to know?"

"Well, first, I want to know if you are *the* Evie,"

Sawyer says. I roll my lips together and narrow my eyes.

"*The* Evie?" I ask. She nods.

"Once, I was asking Julian about Keaton's dating life. In the months that I've known him, I've never seen him talk to, talk about, or even stand near a woman. I asked Julian if he was gay, but he said no. He said he has never been quite the same after Evie. Are you that Evie?"

I love how forward she is.

"Yeah, I guess I am *that* Evie," I say. "I'm not sure if that's good or bad."

She shrugs.

"Me either," she says. "But I'd say that if you're really back, that's probably good."

I smile and nod.

"So tell me," she says, "how did you end up back here with him? Why are you sticking around for the shitshow?"

I laugh. I don't know this girl, but she's been accepted into the tight trust circle of the Everett brothers, so she must be okay. And then I think about how to tell my favorite story of all time: the story of us.

Fifteen Years Ago

EVIE

"Wanna go out to Coney Island?" I ask him as we walk through the halls. It's the last day before our holiday break, and it is absolutely dragging. He doesn't respond. "Keat?"

"Hmm?" he asks. "Oh, yeah, sorry. I, uh..." his voice trails off as we turn down the next hallway. "I'm a little..."

"Bruh," I hear this guy Connor say as soon as he sees us. Well, as soon as he sees Keaton. No one sees me, despite how much I'm with Keaton. I think it's because, around these types of people, most relationships and friendships are superficial. So they assume ours is too. Not worth getting to know me.

Keat sucks in a breath and looks at him.

"Is this true?" he asks, holding his phone out. I see Keaton reading a text message on Connor's phone, but he doesn't say anything. He just walks by.

"That's fucked up, Everett," Connor calls down the hallway. "It's fucked up."

Keaton picks up the pace, and I pick mine up to follow him. My stomach is churning. We turn toward the cafeteria, and Macy walks up to us.

"Keaton, was it really that many people?" she asks. He looks at her, but again, he doesn't answer. He just politely pushes past with me in tow. When we walk into the cafeteria, it feels like a scene from a teen movie. The entire room literally gets quieter. People from every table turn to look at us. Some people are whispering; some are just sitting and staring. Some are glaring, like he just kicked a puppy in front of them.

I don't know what's going on, but my body is screaming at me to do something. I grab his arm and tug him back out of the cafeteria, down the long hall, in the direction of the side door where his security team usually picks us up.

We break out of the doors and through the courtyard, and all the while, I'm clutching onto his hand.

Russ sees us and immediately opens the back door for us to get in. He climbs in the driver's seat and looks at us in the rearview mirror.

"Everything okay, Keaton?" he asks. Keaton doesn't answer. He just sits and breathes. Or maybe not. I think he's hyperventilating.

I turn toward him, throwing my backpack off my shoulders and putting my hands on his.

"Look at me, Keat," I say. He finally does. I mimic long, slow breaths for him, and after a few more sporadic ones, he follows suit. He clutches onto my hands, and I let him.

"Talk to me, Evie," Russ says. "Where am I going? What's going on?"

I look back at Keaton.

"Do you want to go home?" I ask, knowing that's a loaded question. He shakes his head.

"Fuck no."

I think.

"Coney Island?" I ask him.

He shakes his head again.

"No," he says. "No people. I can't... I don't know where—"

"Can you take us to my Nan's, Russ?" I ask. Russ looks at Keaton in the rearview. After a few moments, Keaton nods.

In about twenty minutes, we're pulling up to my Nan's old apartment building. I get out first, looking around for any sign of anyone who might recognize Keaton. But in this neighborhood, that's less likely. He gets out behind me, and I wrap an arm around him as we walk inside. He's never been inside the building, but he doesn't seem to be taking much in right now. I lead him up the five flights of stairs to her door.

I use my key to open it, and when we walk in, she looks up from the newspaper she's reading in her recliner.

"Hi, honey. What are—oh," she says when she sees him. She knows that we're friends. She's the only person I really talk to about it. I've told her about his family, how we spend our time together, how he makes me laugh.

The one thing she never does, though, is ask me about his money. She doesn't ask me if I'm bringing enough to the friendship. Nan is just happy I have someone.

"You must be Keaton," she says, standing up. She walks toward us and brings me in for a hug. Then she looks at him.

"You must be having a very, very long day," she says sincerely. He nods slowly.

"Yes, ma'am," he says. She takes a step forward then slowly wraps him in her arms. And to my absolute shock, he starts to cry. Nan holds him, rubbing his back and patting it. Then, she motions for me to come over to them. I do, and she hands him off to me while she goes to grab some tissues.

So I just stand there in my Nan's apartment, and I hold my big, tall, billionaire best friend while he cries. When he calms down, I had him a wad of tissues. Nan reappears again with two mugs of hot tea, and she leads us further into her living room. I sit down on the couch and motion for him to sit with me. He does, letting out a long breath.

Nan slowly lifts her paper up.

"Does it have anything to do with this?" she asks.

I read the headline.

SEVEN THOUSAND EVERETT ENTERPRISES EMPLOYEES LAID OFF TWO WEEKS BEFORE CHRISTMAS, it reads.

My eyes grow wide.

"Oh, Keat," I whisper, reaching down to squeeze his hand.

"He told us over dinner last night," he says. "So matter-of-factly."

I hold his hand with both of mine.

Nan leans forward in her chair, listening intently.

I'm so glad I have my Nan. I'm so glad to have someone in my life who shows me how to show up for people.

"What did he say?" I ask.

"He just said that they were reallocating some funds on the operations side—whatever that means," he says. "He told us it was necessary so they could expand some other factions of the business. But I think it's some move that's going to cover up the fact that he's paying his rich buddies more."

I bite my lip.

His father is so cruel.

"I just...seven *thousand* employees. That's just...two weeks before Christmas?" he says, pushing himself to stand. "And the worst part is that it included some mid-level executives. Some of whom have kids at our school."

Oh, God.

"Keat, it's not your—"

"I know it's not," he says. "But if I were in their shoes, I'd hate me too."

There's a long pause.

I can't imagine anyone ever hating him. I can't

imagine him ever being deserving of anyone's hatred. The thought alone makes my blood boil.

I scoot forward and stand up, walking over to him.

"It's not your burden to bear, Keaton," I tell him. "I know you want to help them. I know you want to fix this. But this is bigger than you right now. One day, you'll be able to. But right now, let's just play seven card rummy and have some tea. Yeah?"

He sniffs, rubbing his temples between his thumb and pointer finger. Then he looks at me then Nan.

For the next four hours, we sit with Nan, eating, drinking tea, and playing cards. After a while, Nan pulls out her photo albums, and he spends a long while laughing hysterically at pictures of me in my *NSYNC nightgown.

It feels good to see him smile. His laugh does something to me.

And I know in this moment that I would do anything to keep that smile on my best friend's face. The worst part is that he doesn't even know how much joy he brings me. That, on some days, especially when I don't get to see Nan, he is the only source of joy in my life. He's the only person who I can count on. Who makes me feel seen.

And I want to be that for him.

I can't get seven thousand jobs back. I can't help him pay for thousands of holiday gifts. I can't help him with any of that.

But I can remind him that he's not alone in it. And maybe that's worth something too.

He and I are so similar in that way. Both so alone, despite how different our backgrounds are and our journeys to each other were. And yet, when we are together, it doesn't feel lonely. It feels like the missing piece. Like, when nothing else makes sense, he does.

Russ checks in with us every hour.

Cato has apparently been asking for Keat's whereabouts.

Russ has given him our location and has ensured him that we are safe.

That seems to be enough to appease Cato. He is having himself a busy day.

Or, at least, one would think.

Unfortunately, though, according to the news that Nan very quickly turned off, Cato was spotted at one of his golf courses in Florida today. While seven thousand people here are being delivered life-altering news, he's fucking golfing.

Seven thousand people now have to figure out how to make ends meet, how to cultivate the holiday spirit while trying to pay the rent, how to afford healthcare for their loved ones.

But Cato is golfing.

Meanwhile, his kids are still here in the city, bearing the brunt of the anger, bearing the shame of their father, feeling all the feelings that Cato should feel but doesn't.

And I'm going to sit right here with him, feeling it too.

Finally, it's after ten at night, and he sighs.

"I guess I need to go face the music," he says, swiping a hand over his face. Nan stands to give him a hug.

"You can come here anytime, honey. This place is your place too, even if she doesn't come with you. We don't need her," Nan says with a playful wink. He smiles back then looks down at me.

"Yeah, we do."

Present
Day

EVIE

$\mathcal{I}$ finally get to the part of the story where Keaton came to the diner. I get to the part where seeing him for that one moment gave me the strength to ask for help. Where I finally realized that I deserved so much more. And that I didn't have to live like that. When I look at her, sweet Sawyer is crying. She sniffs and wipes her eyes, and I reach out to grab her hand.

"Wow," she says. "I can't imagine being stuck like that," she says. "And of being afraid in your own home."

I swallow.

The fear I let myself live in is something I've felt deeply ashamed of for a very, very long time.

"I hope you're proud of yourself, Evie," Sawyer says. I look up at her. Her big brown eyes are full of hope and wonder. My eyebrows knit together. "You knew you deserved better, and you are finally giving it to yourself."

I give her a nervous chuckle and shrug.

"I don't know about that," I say. "I saw a way out, which ended up being Keaton, and I took it. Not sure that counts as being brave."

She scoots closer to me, putting her hand on mine. And I'm wondering how this woman, who is more than ten years my junior, is making me feel so safe right now. Her eyes bore into mine as she looks at me intently.

"It doesn't matter what finally made you feel safe enough to leave. It just matters that you left. And in that, if you happen to realize what real love looks like, then even better. And if not, then maybe you at least get your new-found-ex-best friend back."

I smile and nod.

"It is good to have him back," I say. "Those Everett boys are really something."

She makes this long-winded, "Mm-hmm," sound as she sips her tea and nestles back into the couch.

"I'm so worried about Julian," she says. "I know he can handle everything in a practical way, but I just don't know if he knows how to handle it emotionally. I'm sure you know better than I do that those boys were never exactly given permission to be vulnerable."

I nod, thinking back to the time I heard Cato tell Keaton he was "weak" for choosing to major in social and environmental studies instead of business or law.

"You got that right," I say. I look at her, lost in her thoughts over Julian. It's sweet, really, watching how much she thinks about him even when he's not near us. And for her to be so much younger but so much more mature when it comes to...well, most things. It's impressive, really. "He's lucky he has you, though. You're right that no one ever gave them permission to be vulnerable. Their mom was as sweet as they come, but unfortunately, when you're married, and then un-married, to the richest man in the world, you don't exactly have equal power when it comes to child-rearing. She did the best she could. But I think—lucky for Julian—that you are doing a pretty good job of picking up where she left off." She looks up at me, one eyebrow raised. I smile. "I've known that man since I was fifteen years old," I tell her. "And not once have I ever seen him display even a minimal amount of affection. He shows his love in other ways. He didn't take his hands off you down there. He is letting himself need you. You're good for him, Sawyer."

She smiles.

"He's good for me too. But I don't know if I will ever get used to this money thing. It's not just like getting a good job, you know? It's like having so much that you can't possibly even wrap your head around it. And maybe that's a good thing. Because who knows how long it will last after this."

I nod.

"Yeah," I say. "But it's up to us to show them that life will go on."

She smiles.

"It sure will."

We spend the next few hours watching episode after episode, when finally, we hear the padding of footsteps coming up the stairs. Sawyer reaches for the remote and turns it down, and we both sit up. Julian and Keaton walk into the room, both looking defeated and exhausted.

"You okay?" Sawyer says, slipping off the couch and making her way to Julian. He lets out a long sigh then wraps himself around her. She strokes the back of his head as she holds him, and it almost makes me teary-eyed. Keaton makes his way to me, and I cup his face in my hands.

"How bad is it?" I whisper. His big gray eyes meet mine.

"Bad," he says. "She brought us written and recorded accounts from a few of the women. I don't even... I can't even bring myself to look at him."

"That's going to be a problem," Julian says. "Because tomorrow is his seventieth birthday party at Bedell House. And we need to be there."

Keaton's eyes snap to Julian.

"You've got to be fucking kidding me," he says. Julian shakes his head.

"Keat, if we don't go, he will know something's up. This has to stay completely under wraps until we have our way out."

Keaton drops his head and blows out a long breath.

"I don't know how the fuck I'm supposed to—"

"You're supposed to think of the women he tricked into working for him and then basically pimped out to his buddies in order to get business. That's how you're supposed to do it," Julian rasps.

"Easy," Sawyer says to him, and I watch as Julian's shoulders immediately drop. I turn to Keaton.

"I'll go with you," I say. His eyes jump back up to mine. "If you want me to. What better a distraction than the girl your dad never liked in the first place?"

This makes him smile, and I feel myself warm a little inside.

"That's a good point," Julian chimes in. "He never liked you. That'll be a good focus for everyone for the night."

Sawyer walks toward us and claps me on the back.

"He hates me too," she says with a smile. "Look at us taking down the patriarchy!"

We laugh, but then I notice the worry in Keaton's eyes. I give his arm a squeeze.

"Let's go home and go to bed," I tell him. He smiles as he looks down at me.

"Home," he says, and it's then that I realize what I just did. I referred to *his* apartment as "home." And while I will spend the rest of the night thinking and overthinking it, I will let him soak it in. I need him to smile. I need him to feel lighter. And I'll do that anyway I can.

KEATON

J don't even remember the drive home. I'm in a daze after what I just heard. What I just read.

Thirty-two women over the course of the last thirty years. Thirty-two women have occupied these made-up executive assistant positions that my father has had created. Thirty-two women have fallen into the trap. Of thinking they are taking a step forward in their career. Of being in need of stability, maybe for themselves, or for their families. Of thinking that Everett Enterprises was the opportunity they had been waiting for.

Ten of those women have come forward to talk to Wren, the reporter for the Manhattan Star. It started with one. One brave woman who decided the secret was getting too heavy to carry with her. And then Wren started to dive in, going undercover, learning that there is a sort of pseudo-community of ex-Everett employees who know each other's secret because they went through the same thing.

I want to find the other twenty. We're working on that now. Julian is having someone he trusts in HR start pulling files, and he's hiring a private investigator to track them all down. If they're dead, we will track down their families. We will do whatever we have to do to take down my father and to make it as right as we can. I know we can't fix the damage he did, but we can at least help them get ready to take on a new day without carrying it. It's such a tangled web—NDAs, statute of limitations, women who have changed their names so as not to be found—but we're working through it. We have to.

And all the while, we have to stay under the radar, keep up the facade that life is going on as we've all known it.

But thinking about having to sit at a table with my father tomorrow night, while hearing those women's terrified voices...it makes me sick.

"He would request that I would join him back at the office after hours. He would pick out an outfit that he would have waiting for me. Sometimes, he would request that I change in front of him. He would often have me join meetings with him and some of his colleagues, though none of them I recognized or could ever find their names in our company directory. Sometimes, he would request that I change in front of them too. Then came the touching. He'd ask me to walk around the board table, letting the men 'feel the fabric' of my dress. It started off with them doing that,

but the more meetings I'd attend, the more comfortable they got."

When Wren asked the woman what happened next, I felt sick.

"There was one time he requested that I meet him at a hotel. I thought we were meeting in a conference room or the lobby, but instead, he had me report to a suite. When I arrived, I found two other men who were waiting for me. When I walked in, one man told Mr. Everett that I would do. When I realized what was about to happen, I turned to leave. Mr. Everett told me that my leaving was a neglect of my duties and would result in immediate termination. When I said I didn't care, he reminded me that I had signed an NDA. As I was fleeing the room, I heard him tell the men not to worry, that he had someone else lined up who would follow through."

It was the "someone else lined up" part that made me especially shiver. Because it meant that he had an open door, a never-ending turnstile of women so that his "supply" never ran out.

My father is a fucking pig.

I feel my fists clench at my sides. I see red. I want to drive to Bendmere, the rambling estate where we grew up. I want to walk past all the gold-encrusted decor in his house and hit him so hard that it makes a Cato-shaped hole in the fucking wall.

But I can't.

Because tomorrow is his motherfucking birthday.

And instead of hitting him, I'll be *celebrating* him.

I blow out a long breath when I feel her warm

hand wrapping around my fists. She gently weaves her fingers through mine, unclenching them, and leans across the seat so she's looking right into my eyes. I take a few breaths, and I feel the weight on my chest start to lift.

"I'm right here," is all she says, and it's all I need to hear.

When we get back to the apartment, she leads the way. She takes my hand and walks me down the hallway to our suite.

"Our" suite.

Even in my most dazed inner thoughts, what's mine is hers.

She goes into the bathroom, and I hear her turn the water on in the tub.

Then she comes back into the room, making a beeline to me. She pulls me to my feet from the bed but doesn't say anything. She slowly, gently starts to undress me. She pulls my shirt up over my head, the chain I wear with my mother's ring falling against my chest.

Then she unbuttons and unzips my jeans, letting them pool at my feet. She tugs down my boxers, and my breath hitches. I feel the blood going straight to my dick, but this doesn't feel sexual—yet. It feels sensual, but like the purpose is innocent. She peels my socks off then leads me into the bathroom to the tub. She motions for me to get in, and I oblige her.

I've never stepped foot in this tub until right now.

I submerge myself into the hot water, and she

adds something to it that smells like vanilla that I didn't even know I had. Then she kneels next to the tub as I lean my head back against the fancy little pillow that the decorator insisted I have—yet another purchase I took for granted and am now thankful for.

Once I close my eyes, I feel a warm cloth dab gently across my chest. I feel her fingers weave through my hair, gently scratching my scalp, and I feel the knots in my stomach loosen up. We don't speak a word. She just washes my body, massages my head, and I just lie here and let her.

When I finally open my eyes, she's staring down at me, her thumb gently stroking my cheek.

"I'd do anything for you, Keaton," she whispers. "I'm sorry it took me so long. But I'm here. And if you'll have me, I'm not leaving you."

Something about this moment, the way I have turned to putty in her hands, how she has me completely naked—in more ways than one—makes those words hit me like a punch to the gut.

"*If I'll have you?*" I ask her. "What on Earth would make you think that was up for debate?"

She clears her throat, her eyes falling down to the water.

"I don't know what... I don't know what kind of future you want. Or if...the kid thing—"

"You, Evie. *You* are the future I want. Full stop."

Her lip quivers as her big green eyes slowly lift back to mine. I stare up at her through narrowed eyes, and I feel a thickness in my chest, crawling up my throat.

I grab her hand and pull it to my lips, closing my eyes and letting myself sit in it all for a moment. I finally open them, and I see that her eyes have tears in them.

"Don't you cry, Evie Dawson," I whisper. "Not when I'm about to."

She lets out a strangled giggle as her voice cracks.

"You don't cry," she says. I let a sad smile show, but our eyes meet again.

"I cry, baby," I tell her, reaching my other hand up to tuck a piece of hair behind her ear. "I cry over you."

Her eyes widen like saucers, and I regret saying it. I wasn't intending to make her feel bad. I just need her to know how much she means to me. What she does to me. What she has always done to me.

I stroke her cheek.

"I need you to stop apologizing to me, Evie," I tell her. "I mean it. You didn't owe me anything then. You don't owe me anything now. You were just a twenty-one-year-old kid making the best decision at the time with the tools you had. No one can fault you for that. It didn't matter if it took one year, eleven years, or if it took thirty more. Shit, it didn't matter if I died before I got to have you, Eve. I was always going to be yours."

She presses up onto her knees and leans over the tub, pressing her lips to mine for a long, hard kiss. I wrap my arms around her, waiting for her to break it off. But she doesn't. Instead, she leans farther over the tub, the fabric of her shirt dipping into the water as she kisses me harder, devouring me. I rub my wet hands up her back, clutching onto her just as tightly. She lets out the softest moan when I bite down gently on her lip.

We finally come apart, and I pull her in even closer, the fabric of her soaked shirt now pierced by hard nipples. I bend down, sucking one through the pink fabric, and she moans again. Then I massage the other before reaching for the hem of her shirt and pulling it up over her head, dropping it in a heavy mound on the tile.

She stands, and I reach up to unzip her jeans and tug them down, along with the red lace panties underneath them. God, I want to fucking devour her.

I wrap my hands around her waist, tugging her back so her thighs are touching the side of the tub. Then I scoot over so my mouth is just inches from her pussy. I slide a finger through her folds, then I flick my eyes up to hers, big, and round, and pleading.

"You're soaked, baby," I whisper, sliding the finger into my mouth. I salivate at her flavor. She moans. "Is this for me?"

She nods wildly, and then I reach around and grab a hold of her ass with both hands.

"Then let me have it," I say just as I dive in. I lick and suck her clit, letting my tongue glide through her folds, my mouth suctioning against her. She writhes beneath me, and I feel her fingernails digging into my shoulders. She hums and moans with pleasure, one hand weaving through my hair and squeezing a fistful of it.

"I need you, Keat," she whispers. "Please."

I hold her to me harder, eating her until her juices are running through my beard, when I feel her legs start to vibrate.

"Please, Keat, I—" she starts, but before she can finish her thought—or her orgasm—I tug her into the tub with me so she's straddling me. I fist my cock and give it a few pumps, then I guide her hips over top of it. Her eyes alight with this need that sets me over the edge, and then she slides down, taking me inch by inch while I lean back against the fancy tub pillow.

She bounces up and down on my dick, the water sloshing all around us, soaking my bathroom floor. But I couldn't give two fucks. I press my fingertips into her hips while she goes, her tits bouncing up and down as she drops her head back. I run one hand up her stomach, pressing it between her breasts, holding her steady so she keeps hitting the spot she needs.

She moans and screams my name, one hand slapping down on the cool ceramic, the other pressing down on my chest. She rocks back and forth, and I give my hips a slight lift.

"That's it, baby," I growl. "Just hold it steady for me. I'll get you there."

She lets out a low moan, dropping her head back. Her long red locks spill into the water as I fuck her, and I'm not letting up. I feel her thighs tighten around me, and when I know she's close, I slide my hand down. I press gently against the bottom of her stomach and add a little bit of pressure to her clit until I feel her whole body lock up. I have my release, spilling myself into her just as she collapses onto me. We sit like this for a few moments, her forehead against my chest, my hands running up and down her sides gently as we both come down. Finally, we have enough energy to get out of the tub and into the shower, and it's my turn to wash her.

We get out, dry off, but elect to stay naked, getting into my bed and curling up into each other. I love the way she smells. Her hair, her skin. Everything about her pulls me in, and I am so sick of fighting it. I just want to hold her like this until the end of fucking time.

One last moment where I don't know where she begins and where I end.

Then I could die a happy man.

EVIE

There are so many things about this party that make me anxious that I'm not sure I can name them all.

First, there is the fact that I'm seeing his family—his whole family—again. The first time since my early twenties. When we were kids, we ironically didn't spend a whole lot of time with the Everetts, which my other friends thought was crazy.

I remember Annie Cramer asking me in homeroom once what the point of having a billionaire friend was if I didn't take advantage of any of the perks.

The truth was, I forgot he was rich.

Often.

He didn't cruise around Manhattan in a chariot. He didn't stick with his security detail. He didn't parade around penthouses. Instead, he preferred to assimilate into my life when we were together. We hung at my house, and his security waited outside. We went to Coney Island. We went to coffee shops.

Perk of being the second-born Everett was that most people only recognized Cato and Julian. Keaton was the "spare" as he so affectionately referred to himself. Julian was the "heir" in the public eye. He was the oldest, looked the most like Cato, and was in line to take over all the family businesses.

Then when Brooks came along, his birth in and of itself was a scandal that attracted all the media. For years, they'd stalk around, trying to get pictures of him.

Keaton was able to hide away, using the middle-child thing to his advantage. We would go to Bedell House, the Everett family estate, only when he knew that his family wasn't going to be on property, when we could have it to ourselves. We would run through the gardens, fish in the pond, hide out in the library.

I met Cato a few times throughout my friendship with Keaton, and though he was polite on paper, he was snarky and sarcastic and never showed interest in anyone for too long. I particularly despised the way he made Keaton the butt of so many of his jokes once it became apparent that he wasn't going to follow Julian's footsteps and go to business school.

And as we got older, we hung around them less and less.

The next item of anxiety is the fact that I have to not only see them, but I have to act like everything is normal. And the problem is, I don't know what *normal* is anymore. Normal *feels* like Keaton. Being with him feels normal. Natural. It requires absolutely no thinking on my part, which is why being with him feels so freeing. Brain off, feelings on.

But to anyone on the outside, nothing about this situation is normal.

Twenty years ago, we were inseparable, but we never belonged to each other.

Then I got married.

Keaton left and never came back.

Until now.

Now, he's back.

Now, I'm getting divorced.

In the span of a few days, I've left my marriage and shacked up with my billionaire ex-best friend.

That can't look good.

But it has to look *normal.*

And being that I don't know which way is up, I definitely don't know which way is normal.

I just know which way to go to get to him.

Sawyer sent me to some store uptown where she now gets her wardrobe made. She says it's the only thing she lets herself splurge on, because she can finally find clothes that fit her. Clothes that make her *feel* good.

Our bodies are very different. She's taller, slimmer, straighter—younger, I remind myself.

I've worked hard to love myself for my entire adult life, but it's been double the work lately. When you don't see your worth, having someone to remind you what they see can be life-altering. Empowering. Freeing.

But having someone remind you that you're not worth anything can be damaging in ways that feel like they will never be fixed. Having someone solidify the ugly thoughts you have about yourself make them that much harder to ignore.

I'm on my way back, though. I'm letting myself have things I think I deserve. Not just deserve—*want*. I'm making decisions based on *me*. I'm getting little pieces of myself back that I wasn't sure I'd see again.

So having a dress be specifically fitted to my body? Wearing something that feels like it was made just for me?

I'm going to let myself have that.

And boy, did I.

Aaron, the stylist, matched tones and colors and fabrics to me. He talked to me about necklines and hemlines and some other kind of lines. He had me stand in front of a few mirrors while he tested some dresses out under different lighting.

And then he wrapped me in this emerald-green dress that he said matched my eyes, and I felt like Cinderella had just left her fairy godmother.

I have never felt more beautiful than I do in this dress.

Except for maybe when Keaton drags those eyes over my body.

Aaron picked out a pair of strappy nude sandals with a wide enough heel that I feel confident in my ability to walk in them and a matching nude clutch. The final piece was a shimmery nude shawl, and he sent me on my way.

Now, I'm sitting in the bathroom of Keaton's guest suite, having my hair done by a professional that Sawyer also recommended and a makeup artist who is currently putting on so much mascara I'm worried if I close my eyes, I won't be able to open them again.

When they both step away from me, I do a double-take.

The fabric has this give to it that makes me feel sexy. It hugs my body in all the places that Keaton has kissed. All the places he refuses to let me hide.

They have done my hair in an elegant updo, one of those that looks strategically messy on purpose, and my makeup is flawless.

I swallow as they exit the bathroom and make their way down the hall, saying their goodbyes to Keaton as they leave. I appear at the end of the hall-way, and I see him talking to Mac, looking as dazzling as ever in his perfect fucking suit.

Fuck the gown, the suit, the makeup, the hair. All of it.

I just want to fuck *him*.

I draw in a breath as his eyes find me, scanning me from head to toe, his tongue jutting out to lick his lips. Then they tug up into this dangerously sexy half-smile as he walks toward me, meeting me in the middle.

"Jesus, you're perfect," he whispers. He bends down to leave a soft, careful kiss on my lips.

"Little more flattering than my usual sweats and flannel, huh?" I ask, visibly uncomfortable. He knows how bad I am at accepting compliments. But he doesn't waver. He reaches his hand out and takes one of mine, lifting it to his lips.

"Sweetheart, there is no such thing as unflattering when it comes to you," he says. "There is no version of you that doesn't melt me into a fucking puddle."

I giggle and roll my eyes, but his expression doesn't change.

I'm not used to this full, undivided attention he gives me, and I don't quite know what to do with it. "This dress is beautiful. It was made for you. I want to *be* this dress. Be wrapped around you like this. My next favorite is when you're wearing something of mine. You're comfortable, but you're claimed. You're all mine." I smile, staring up into his big gray eyes, listening intently. "But, no questions asked, hands down, my favorite is when you're naked in my bed."

I laugh, but then I realize, he's not kidding.

"I'm serious," he says. "I love every single inch of your body, Evie Dawson. It's even better than I ever could have imagined. And I imagined it plenty." Then he pulls me in for another kiss, expertly kissing me so that my makeup stays intact. "Now, let's go before I rip this thing off of you."

"That doesn't sound so bad," I whisper back with a smile. His hand slides down and gently taps my ass.

"Don't tempt me, Dawson," he says, his voice low and gritty and making me squeeze my legs together. We get on the elevator, get in the car, and make the drive out to Bedell House.

When we pull up, a little under an hour later, I'm a bit shellshocked. Mac types a code in at the huge iron gates, his hand is scanned, and then the gates open, and we start up the extra-long driveway. I remember Keaton once telling me that the driveway itself was a mile long. And as we approach, I forgot how fucking massive this place is. How perfectly manicured it is. The huge stone palace sits on this tract of land on Long Island that Keaton's great-great grandfather had built once they struck oil. His family lived here for decades until Cato decided to build his own estate, Bendmere, about thirty miles out.

When Keaton's grandpa died, he left the house to the family in the will with the agreement that public tours would still be permitted, and no unnecessary updates, additions, or changes would be made to the property.

Mac pulls the car up around the circle to the big front doors and puts the car in park. He zooms around to grab our door, but Keaton is already out of the car, holding a hand out for me. He helps me slide out, straightening out the bottom of my gown for me then giving me his arm.

"You ready?" he asks me. I look up at him, our eyes locking, and for the first time since we decided to come here together, I feel confident. I do feel ready, because Keaton needs me to be. So that's what I'll be. I nod and smile, squeezing his hand.

"Let's do this," I tell him, and he leads me up the big, over-the-top stone staircase that leads to the main doors. Two doormen exit the building, holding open the big, cathedral-style doors and waving us inside. Keaton greets both of them with a smile, leading me through the doors.

I draw in a long, slow breath as I take in Bedell House, refamiliarizing myself with it. It looks largely the same. Everything is massive and looks untouched despite the thousands of people that walk these halls every year. He leads me farther into the house, and there are people everywhere, carrying trays of drinks and hors d'oeuvres. There are big, beautiful rose bouquets on every table, and music fills the halls, sweeping its way down to us from the grand hall, which I remember is in the west wing. There are guests standing around, sipping their drinks at the cocktail tables, ordering from one of the four bars that are set up around the main level, chatting with each other and looking like they absolutely fit in here.

I don't, but I never really felt like Keaton did either.

I think that's what gave me hope for us in the first place.

And then Cato squashed it.

But that was then.

This is now.

And now, Keaton needs me. He *wants* me. He has chosen me, and there is nothing Cato Everett can do about it.

Keaton leads me into a smaller room off the grand

hall that doesn't feel any less grand. I remember the huge three-story fireplace. This is where the Everett's family tree was set up every year, not to be confused with the forty-foot one they set up in the main foyer for guests. Back in the day, Keaton's grandfather would select five charities or non-profits, and then visitors could make a small donation to one of their choosing. When they donated, they would get an ornament that they could add to the tree.

When his grandfather died, Cato did away with the tradition. He told the boys that they weren't in the business of playing "banker" and collecting money for other "businesses." I remember Keaton drank himself silly that night in my bedroom.

When we walk in, the first person I lay eyes on is Sawyer, and I am instantly at ease. Maybe misery loves company, but I know Cato doesn't like her and thinks she's a "gold-digging bimbo," as she so eloquently put it. I also know from Keat that she put Cato on blast in front of all his rich buddies at his wife's birthday party a few months ago. So she might be one of my new favorite people.

Keaton tightens his grip on me as he leads me through the crowd, smiling and nodding politely at all the people who stare at us, just craving any attention he will give them. I hate that for him because I know *he* hates it. He wants to be as far away from Bedell House as he can be.

Just as we approach them, I hear someone from behind us.

"Well, well, well," the voice says, but I don't recognize it. "Who do we have here, big brother?"

We spin back around, and I see a much taller, broader, much more handsome Brooks. His eyes grow wide when he sees my face and realizes that it's me. His eyes bounce from me to Keaton, over to Julian, and back to me.

"Do my eyes deceive me, or has the girl who crushed my brother's heart waltzed back into our lives?" he asks me with a coy smile. There is a beautiful blonde on his arm, who is looking around the room, sipping a glass of champagne. She doesn't belong here either—I can tell. But she is pretty desperate for no one to know.

I smile back at him just as I feel Keaton tense up next to me.

"That's because I heard that his pain-in-the-ass little brother wasn't around much, but I guess I was the one who was deceived," I say. Sawyer scoffs from behind us, and Keaton and Julian choke back laughs. Brooks raises an eyebrow but smiles down at me as he looks between us again.

"So you're back, then, huh?" he asks. I nod and smile.

"You can't get rid of me this time," I tell him. He looks at Keaton, then looks back at me, then takes a step toward me and pulls me in for a hug.

"In that case, get in here," he says. I hug him back, but it lasts longer than I'm prepared for. He rubs my back gently and makes a soft humming noise, like he's eating something he likes. When I realize what he's doing, I let go of him, just as Keaton playfully shoves him off.

"Nice try, dick," Keaton says. Brooks backs away with an innocent shrug.

"Hey, I was just a tyke when she dipped," he says. "She might want to make sure she's chosen the right brother." At that, the blonde whips her head around to us.

Keaton rolls his eyes, and I put my hand on Brooks's shoulder.

"Aww, nice try, Brooksy," I say, "but you are forever ingrained in my brain as the kid who pissed himself on the Ferris wheel. You are forever eight in my mind, honey."

This makes Julian laugh out loud, which I consider a win. He's so much more serious than the other two. It's nice to break down that wall. When the blonde realizes I am not a threat, she turns her head back to the crowd, back to people-watching.

Brooks takes his defeat like a man, laughing along with his brothers.

"Alright, alright," he says. "So, what is this, then? Didn't you ditch the Everetts to go get hitched or something?"

"Who says 'hitched' anymore?" Sawyer pipes in, and I love her.

"Brooks, give it a rest," Keaton says, but I rub his arm, letting him know I can handle whatever wrench is thrown at me today. If getting through today means being the butt of the jokes and the center of the Everett family gossip, then so be it.

"I did, Brooks," I say, matter-of-factly. "But I think I knew all along where I was actually supposed to be. Just had to find my way back." I look up at Keaton and wink, and he smiles down at me.

"Well, I, for one, am glad you're here. I need some more dirt on these guys. More collateral for blackmail, ya know?" Sawyer says with a big grin, holding her glass in the air. I nod my head in her direction.

"Happy to be of service," I say with a wink. Julian wraps an arm around her waist and smiles.

"I'm glad too," he says with a sincerity in his eyes that feels foreign to me. "We all need our people right now."

Brooks looks at his brothers, eyebrows raised. They don't say anything, just shoot him a look that says, "you should have showed up." But before Brooks can ask anything, the lights in the room flicker, and the music gets louder.

"Here he comes," Julian warns, throwing the rest of his beer back before putting it on a tray that's being carried by. I see him reach for Sawyer's hand, and I interlock my fingers with Keaton's.

"I'm here," I whisper as his grip on me tightens.

But as his eyes narrow in on his father with a look of pure disgust, I don't know if he is.

KEATON

"*L*adies and gentlemen, the man of the hour, the man of the house, Cato Everett!" the MC says, and the crowd erupts like they are at a fucking concert.

I look around at them, wondering how many of them know. How many of them are involved with it. I know certain members of the board were at the "meetings." I've had my eyes on them since I walked in the house. Fucking pigs.

I'm so mad, so disgusted at what my father has become—or maybe, what he always was. I just chose not to see it. He walks down the grand staircase like a fucking king, his third wife clung to his arm like an expensive piece of art. He waves at his admirers, people whose loyalty he has bought over the decades. They clap and wave and laugh and smile like the blind followers they are, and it's not until Evie taps my hand that I realize how tightly I'm clutching on to her.

How hard I'm gritting my teeth. How shallow my breaths are. How much pure hatred is radiating off of me.

"Breathe," she whispers. "It's his birthday, remember?"

I draw in a few long breaths, blowing them out slowly.

Calm down, Keaton. Play this off.

I nod back at her, looking down into those big green eyes. I feel my jaw unclench as she kisses the back of my hand. Cato takes the microphone, and I feel myself go rigid again. I look at my brother, but he is strong, collected, stoic.

Be like Julian.

"Thank you all so much for being here tonight," Cato says, and the crowd claps. "Angelina and I really are so grateful for each and every one of you. Everett Enterprises has never been more lucrative than it has been over the last decade. We are constantly growing, even when the rest of the world is stagnant."

How like him to turn a birthday celebration into a fucking commercial and to toot his own fucking horn.

"But more than that, we are blessed to be standing here with our family." He turns to us, raising a glass. "Boys, there is no greater joy in my life than getting to be your father. I am so proud of each of you, and I rest easy at night, knowing that the Everett legacy will carry on because of you."

My brothers and I look at each other, and I freeze. I feel nauseated. Julian raises his glass, and Brooks does the same. Evie nudges me, and I finally will my hand to follow suit. The room erupts with applause again.

"Still waiting on some grandchildren, though!" he adds, and the room bursts into whoops and laughter. We look at each other awkwardly, Julian feigning a smile and Brooks running a hand over his neck playfully. I take another swig of my drink. Jesus Christ. *Grandchildren.* If I have kids, they may never know this man.

If I can help it.

"But seriously," Cato goes on, "thank you all for joining me to celebrate. Here's to the next decade!" The crowd erupts again, and the five of us turn back to our table. Brooks's date just looks on, completely unaware of anything that is being communicated amongst us. The head waiter approaches us.

"Pardon the interruption, but dinner will be served shortly. Your father has reserved your seats at the head table."

"We need an extra seat," Julian says. The waiter looks at me then nods.

"Yes, of course, Mr. Everett. Please follow me."

"Think we know the way, there, big guy," Brooks says, putting an empty beer bottle on the table. "But thanks." He flips an imaginary cap. The waiter walks away, and Julian turns to him.

"Don't be a dick," he says.

"Yeah. It's not his fault. None of this is," I growl.

Brooks holds his hands up.

"Chill out, dudes," he says. "Lighten up."

I whip around to him.

"Maybe if you ever took anything fucking seriously, you would realize what the fuck is going on here," I quip. His eyes grow wide.

"Easy," Julian warns under his breath. "Now is not the time. Smiles on. Show time."

We walk into the main hall, and I can't help but notice what feels like every single head turning in our direction as we go. The event photographer snaps photos of us, and I feel Evie sliding behind me. I look down at her, but she just smiles back up at me. I tighten my hold on her hand. We get to the table as the servers are finishing setting up the additional seat. I know that was probably a big fucking deal. These things are planned down to the last fucking morsel of food. The last ice cube. Gift baskets for every guest in attendance. So it tickles me a bit to disrupt it.

Julian takes the chair next to the head where my father and Angelina will sit. I can't stand Angelina, but if anyone can't stand her even more, it's Brooks. So I decide to be a good big brother and take the seat next to her, pulling out Evie's chair before I sit. Brooks sits on the other side of her, his date on the other side of him.

After a few more agonizing moments, Cato and Angelina approach the table.

"My boys," he says, clapping his hands together. We all stand, and he hugs us one by one, Angelina following suit, until he gets to Evie, and I feel my pulse quicken.

"My, my, my," he whispers, staring down at her. "Genevieve Dawson? Is that you?"

She swallows and nods.

"Hi, Mr. Everett," she says. She sticks a hand out to shake his, but instead, he takes it softly, bringing it to his lips, his eyes locked on hers. I fight every urge in my body to yank her from his grasp.

"To what do we owe the pleasure of seeing you again after all these years?" he asks ever so smoothly. My heart is pounding in my chest. Every inner thought is yelling at me, screaming for me to take her and run. But I stand still.

"Keaton," she says matter-of-factly, looking up at me with a smile that could fucking bring me to my knees. I know he's looking for more, but she doesn't offer it. She just stares up at me, smiling, letting me know she's got this. Cato's eyes bounce back and forth between us, but he decides against pressing the matter at his birthday party. Instead, he invites us all to sit just as the wait staff begins bringing out the first course.

Dinner goes off fairly easily. A video montage plays that takes up a good chunk of it, filled with photos that make Cato look like the most loving father and greatest philanthropist in the world. I can't help but notice how no photos appear that show my mom or Brooks's, despite them giving Cato the heirs to his kingdom.

After the montage, video messages from his

celebrity friends that couldn't be in attendance play, and I throw back another sip of my beer.

As the final course is taken away, I let out a breath, knowing that this will all be over soon—until my father claps his hands together.

"Okay, boys, one more favor," he says. "Portrait time."

My eyes flick to Julian then to Brooks.

"Come again?" Julian asks.

"We haven't had a family portrait taken in years. Not since Angelina and I got married." Angelina beams next to him, and I roll my eyes. Evie kicks me under the table. "As a birthday present to me, I'd like to get one taken tonight, while everyone is so dressed up."

I look at my brother, waiting for his lead. He clears his throat then nods.

"Sure, Cato. It's your day," he says. We all stand slowly, and I make eyes at Evie. She just nods and smiles.

"I'll be right here," she says.

As we follow Cato and Angelina out of the main hall and down toward the fireplace, Cato turns to me.

"You know what would be the best birthday gift ever?" he asks me. I look at him. "If you would come back to New York. I have some projects I think you would—"

"You're getting your portrait, Dad," I say coldly. "Let's not push it."

Julian glares at me, and I clear my throat as the photographer directs us all where to stand.

"Right," Cato says, a stiff smile on his lips.

"Cool down," Julian growls at me under his breath. We pose for what feels like four hundred photos, any sense of a genuine smile diminishing with each one. When we finally get back to the main hall, I plop down in the seat next to Evie, my shoulders immediately lowering.

She reaches a hand up and cups the back of my neck, pulling me down to her.

"Why don't we take a quick break?" she whispers. I raise an eyebrow. She bites her lip. "I might not be wearing any panties."

I can't fight the smile.

This girl.

I look around. People are finishing their food and starting to mingle more. The room is getting more crowded, and more importantly, my brothers are preoccupied with entertaining other people. I stand up, take her hand, and practically yank her from the table.

I lead her out of the main hall, smiling and nodding at people as we go, then turn down one of the longer corridors that heads to the family wing. My grandfather had the family wing renovated when he decided to open the house up for tours so that we always had a place in Bedell House that was just ours. But I'm skipping the sentimentalities tonight. I bypass our wing, heading up one of the side staircases until we reach the west garden doors. I type in a code before exiting so the alarms don't trigger, and we slip out. I lead her out onto the terrace then down the big stone steps to the garden path. I bend down to scoop her up, and she giggles.

"Careful!" she cries. "I'm not as light as I used to be."

I glare at her in my arms.

"You're gonna pay for that comment," I tell her before busting into a light jog through the

garden until I reach my destination: the pool house.

I type another code in on the door, open it, and step inside, bolting it behind us.

I set her down, eyeing her fully for the first time. I let my eyes scour her body from head to toe again, really taking her in, letting myself revel in just her—no cameras, no Cato, no anybody else.

"Now," I say, taking a step toward her, "what was that you were saying?"

She swallows, biting her bottom lip.

"Just that I...I'm not as..." she says, her throat bobbing. I step closer to her so our chests are touching. I bend down so my lips are just centimeters from her neck. I cup the back of her head, tilting it back farther.

"Not as...what?" I ask. I drag my lips up and down the length of her neck without letting them touch her skin. She swallows again but doesn't speak. "That's what I thought," I tell her. "Stop talking about my woman the way you've been talking about her. Do you understand me?"

She looks up at me, eyes wide.

"This body," I say, my hands moving up and down her sides, her hips, her ass, "this *perfect* fucking body, belongs to me. And no one, not even you, will talk about it that way. So now, you'll sit here while I take every inch of it, until you see it the way I do. Understand?"

She nods again slowly as I reach up and grab the skinny little silk straps of her dress, tugging them down her shoulders. I spin her around, undoing her clasp and zipper slowly, leaving little kisses down her spine that make her bend backward.

When I get the zipper to the tip of her ass, I realize she wasn't bluffing. No panties on my girl. Easy access.

"That's my dirty little girl," I whisper in her ear as I tug the fabric off over her hips. "No panties for me? Were you hoping I'd get you alone like this?"

She doesn't say anything just lets out a quiet moan and nods.

I spin her back around, reaching to unclasp the strapless bra she's wearing. Her perfect tits spill out, and I reach a hand up to cup one, squeezing it so I can gently suck her nipple into my mouth. She moans again, biting her bottom lip.

"I'm thinking I might need to teach you a lesson for that little comment you made," I say, moving over to her other breast, nibbling on her nipple before sucking it into my mouth. "What do you think?"

She nods again.

I take her hand gently, leading her across the room

to the large couch that sits in the center. I take a seat, then I pat my lap.

"Lie down," I tell her.

She swallows, but she listens.

She crawls across my lap, face down, ass up. I feel my cock stiffening beneath her. I palm her ass gently before pulling back and giving her a light, smooth tap. She moans under my hand.

"You're not going to talk about yourself like that anymore, right?"

She shakes her head. I smack her ass again. "I can't hear you, Evie. Use your words."

"No," she breathes.

"Good," I tell her. "That's a good girl. Because we don't say anything about this beautiful, round ass other than how perfect it is, right?" She nods, and I spank her again. "Right?"

"Right," she says.

I nod.

"Good girl," I say. I reach a hand underneath her and flip her onto her back, sliding out from under her. I crawl up her body, caging her in between my arms. "And we don't say anything about these tits," I say, taking one into my mouth again, "unless it's about how fucking perfect and perky they are. How perfectly they fit in my hands. Right?"

"Right." She nods, her cheeks flushing.

"And this," I say, sliding my hands down her sides and placing one on her stomach. "This beautiful stomach," I say, kissing one side of her belly button then the other. "We don't say anything about it unless it's about how fucking beautiful it is. How safe and comfortable it makes me feel when I lie on it. How it feels like home."

Her eyes widen as she stares up at me.

"Right?" I ask her. She nods shyly.

"And this," I say, sliding my hand down to cup her pussy. She hisses and presses her head back into the couch cushion. I slide one finger in and out of her folds, gliding through her juices. "This pretty fucking pussy," I growl. "What do we say about this pretty pussy?"

"We say that it's all yours," she breathes, writhing, pushing into my touch further.

EVIE

"That's right," he says, slipping his finger out of me. He reaches back to undo his pants, and I reach up to help him, getting his slacks and shirt off in record time. He lowers himself back down, lining himself up with my entrance, and pushes inside of me. I scream out, smacking one hand against the couch and the other against his chest.

"Take a breath, baby," he says. "You know we will make it fit."

I hum as he moves farther and farther in, filling me to the hilt. He waits a beat for me to adjust then grabs my hips and begins moving. He fucks me slow at first, his hands still worshipping my body.

"You are so fucking beautiful, Evie," he says. "So pretty. And you take me so fucking well."

God, the mouth on him is so much dirtier than I remember. And I fucking love it.

But then I remember that this whole tryst was my

idea. And it's supposed to be for *him*—not that there isn't some reward in it for me too.

I let him move in and out of me a few more strokes before I push up onto my elbows, shoving him backward. He falls back, shooting me a confused look. I smile as I crawl onto him, straddling him.

"It's my turn," I tell him before sliding down his length, letting him fill me back up. I rock back and forth slowly at first then quicker once I find our rhythm. He grabs hold of my hips again, moving me how he wants me.

"Bad girl," he whispers through a smile that I swear could make me come on its own. I ride him faster, picking up the pace. I run my hand through his hair, tugging it gently and tilting his head back, exposing his neck to me. I lean in, kissing and licking it in tiny little circles, and he lets out a throaty groan. I bite him gently, and he grips my hips harder.

"You better be careful, Eve," he says.

I lean back, giving him a daring look as I bounce up and down on his dick.

"Or what?" I challenge him. He doesn't say anything, so I lean forward, licking a long line up the side of his neck again before I dive in and take another bite. He lets out a growl before pushing to stand, me still on his cock. He slides me off with little effort then turns me around, putting me down on the couch on my stomach. He grabs my hips again, pulling my ass up in the air to him. He licks his hand, rubbing it against my pussy before he shoves himself back into me from behind.

"Yes, Keat," I breathe, clutching onto the couch cushion. "Use me. Fuck me until it's all out of your system."

He moves quicker, faster, harder, grunting behind me as he does. He reaches a hand around, pressing his fingers against my clit and rubbing in slow circles while he fucks me. I start to come undone just as he does, and then I feel his body go rigid then give way as he lowers his weight on top of me. He keeps fucking till I explode, and we both fall onto the couch. Once he catches his breath, he flips me over to face him.

"Thank you for that," he says, leaning over to kiss me. "But just so we're clear, I will never fuck you just to use you."

I put my hand on his face.

"Keat, you know what I meant," I say. "I just wanted—"

"I know, honey," he cuts me off. "And it worked. But I will never fuck you and it not mean something. And I will never, *ever* get you out of my system."

We get dressed and clean ourselves up bit, and he waits for me to attempt to fix my hair and makeup, which is a joke.

"Ready?" I ask him when I come back into the room. He smiles.

"I'm ready."

. . .

THE REST of the night goes off with nothing really to report. We mostly hang with Julian and Sawyer, Brooks dropping in now and then. He doesn't mind the social climbing as much. He is still basking in the fruits of his family's labor.

Around eleven, Julian and Keaton give each other a look.

"I think three hours is enough to punch our time-card," Julian says. "Shall I call the cars?"

Sawyer scoffs.

"God, you sound like a rich prick when you say shit like that." She giggles, a little bit wine tipsy. He shoots her a playful glare before leaning in to playfully pinch her sides.

"Watch it, baby girl," he says, and Keaton makes a playful puking sound behind them.

We say our goodbyes and go surprisingly unnoticed as we make our way out to the driveway. Sawyer gives me a big hug goodbye, and we get in our separate cars and make our way back to the city.

When we get back, Mac pulls the car around to the gate, when I stop him.

"I want pancakes," I say.

Keaton looks at me, raising an eyebrow. Then he smiles.

"Can you take us to the diner, Mac?"

"Sure thing, boss," he says, flipping a U and heading back in that direction.

We get there about ten minutes later, and Mac drops us off at the door while he finds parking. I walk through the doors, my gown and heels raising some looks from the late-night customers as we walk inside. Sean, the cook, sees me first and lets out a long whistle.

"Well, look at what the cat dragged in," he says, "and dressed so nice!"

I laugh and make my way toward him for a hug. I turn and reach an arm out for Keaton.

"This is Keaton," I say. Sean's eyes are wide as he shakes his hand.

"Mr. Everett," he says. "It's a pleasure. What can we get for you all?"

"Nice to meet you, Sean," Keaton says with that panty-dropping smile that dropped my panties just a few hours ago. "I think we will just take two stacks of pancakes, yeah?"

I nod enthusiastically as Sean leads us to an empty booth toward the back. Within minutes, we are laughing and stuffing our faces with diner pancakes like we didn't stuff our faces with a gourmet meal just a few hours back. I get up to refill our drinks behind the counter, but when I turn back, I freeze.

Because my motherfucking husband is staring back at me.

KEATON

The hair on the back of my neck instantly stands up when I notice the look on her face.

Fear.

I whip my head toward the front door of the diner, and I see him.

The same bastard who convinced her she wasn't worthy. Who made her feel guilty for

not being able to get pregnant. Who put his fucking *hands* on her.

The same bastard I warned to stay the *fuck* away from her unless she reached out to him. And there's no way she did.

Did she?

I stand up, and I see him look at me out of the corner of his eye. But he doesn't turn in my direction. He keeps his eyes on her. Her eyes flit to me for a brief moment then back to him.

"Tanner," she says. "What...what are you doing here?"

He glares at her, and as I get closer to her, I can see his eyes are glassy and bloodshot. His skin looks clammy, and it's not till I get closer to him that I see what's in his hand.

I can see the divorce papers shaking in his clutch.

"I came to see if you were done fucking around yet," he says. "So you just have these delivered like I'm your fuckin' pen pal, and then you dip out to play house with the rich kid?" he asks her. "It took you all of one night with him to let him convince you to do this?" His voice stays calm and even, and I see her swallow. I take a step toward her, but she holds her hand out, stopping me.

"Tanner," she says again, her voice also staying cool and even, "this isn't the place."

"Yeah, well," he says, "I can't seem to get to you anywhere else. So here will have to do."

She looks around.

There are only four other people in the diner besides Sean and the cook. But they are still witnesses. He doesn't look particularly dangerous. He just looks drunk and a little sad. But I still want to punch his fucking face in.

She takes a breath, and I see something shift in her. She looks at me, and then it's like I can see something click in her head. She pushes past him and out the door, back onto the sidewalk. He follows after her, and I am right on his tail. When she gets outside, she turns back to him. She flits her eyes back up to him and takes two steps in his direction. I instinctively move closer to her, but I try to be respectful of her wishes. I fight every single instinct in my body not to grab her and pull her behind me.

"Tanner, no one convinced me to do anything, except for you," she says. His eyes grow wider, then he narrows them on her. "I shouldn't have let you tear me down year after year like I did. But I did. I loved you once, Tanner. But we were different people then. I never thought you were someone who would try to make me feel smaller. But you did. And it's time for me to be free of that. I won't live my life in fear anymore. Not of you coming home shitfaced. Not of you hurting me. Not of you making me feel like I'm less than. You made me afraid to be the biggest, best version of myself. And that is over. I can't stop you from going down, but I can save myself from being dragged down with you."

He just stares back at her. One eye twitches slightly, like he's trying to fight back tears.

"I'm not giving you a fucking penny," is all he can muster up. She lets her lips turn up into a sweet smile.

"If you knew me at all, you'd know that that doesn't mean a goddamn thing to me. Keep it all. Everything. I don't want a single thing that reminds me of you, Tanner. I am freeing myself of you. It's yours."

He scoffs.

"Yeah, I fuckin' bet. You got a new man to foot all

the bills and then some for the rest of your fuckin' life. Till he gets sick of your ass and puts you out like I should have," he says, stumbling backward. She just smiles up at him, despite the fact that I am about to combust next to her.

"You motherfu—" I start, but she puts a hand against my chest, pushing me back.

"Whatever you have to tell yourself while you're sleeping in our bed alone, Tanner," she says to him. Then, she turns back to me and puts her hand on my cheek. "Take me home."

I nod, wrapping an arm around her.

If I wasn't boiling over with anger, I'd be beaming with pride right now. I'm so fucking proud of her.

We turn to walk toward the car when I freeze, not able to help myself. I turn back to him, and he is just staring at us.

"Tanner," I call back to him, "just so we're clear, if she ever leaves me, it'll be on her own account. Whatever's mine is hers for as long as she wants it. I'm not dumb enough to fumble her."

I turn back to her, and she shoots me a "you shouldn't have" look, but I can see that she's fighting a smile. When we get in the car, she turns to me.

"You just couldn't help yourself, huh?" she says. I smile and lean forward, stealing a kiss from her lips.

"Sorry," I say. "I had to. But you were fucking phenomenal, baby. He's going to be replaying that in his head for years."

She laughs and lays her head on my shoulder. But

after a moment, I become starkly aware that her entire demeanor has changed. I nudge her gently, and she tips her head up to me. I see tears in her eyes.

"What is it, baby?" I whisper, cupping her face in my hand. She sniffs and shakes her head, forcing a little smile. I just stroke her cheek with my thumb, waiting for her to be ready. My stomach churns. Should I have kept my mouth shut? Or—god help me —is she worried she made some sort of mistake?

She wraps her hand around my wrist. I take a long breath.

"I'm so...I'm so relieved," she says. "I'm so proud of myself for saying all of that. But I'm still so mad that it took me so long. What was I...what was I thinking? How could I...how could I let someone make me feel so small?"

My heart splinters in my chest.

I want to turn the car around, get out, and deck him.

Fuck that guy. Fuck everything he ever did and said to her that made her feel anything less than fucking perfect.

"Oh, sweetheart," I whisper, leaning forward to kiss her forehead. I hold my lips to her for a few seconds, as if I'm willing the sadness to leave her body. I remember this feeling. I remember being so angry with myself when I finally got out of the city, when I finally felt like I was out of my dad's clutch, when his words of disappointment in me finally dissipated the longer I stayed the fuck away from him.

And I remember the shame. How angry I was with myself for letting him hold onto me, digging his claws in so deep.

It took me years and a lot of therapy to finally forgive myself. To comfortably place the blame on *him*. To come to terms that the responsible party was my father.

It didn't happen overnight. And it won't for her either. There will be a voice in her head that will try and drag her back down.

But I'll be louder.

I'll be the voice that fights back until she's ready to do it herself.

And I make a silent promise to both of us in this moment that she will never feel anything but loved, cherished, and safe with me. She will feel like she is enough, because she's so, so much more. She is everything. She always has been.

I tip her head back up to me again, swiping her tears away from her eyes.

"You were just surviving, baby," I tell her. "You were doing what you had to do to get by. I know it doesn't feel like it right now, but you will realize it. And you will forgive yourself. And until you do, I'll be here to remind you of everything that you deserve. Because it's the fucking world, Evie."

She looks up at me, tear-filled eyes now showing signs of something else: hope.

And if I give her nothing else, let it be that.

EVIE

A few weeks have passed since Cato's party and our run-in with Tanner. My lawyer got word that he agreed to mediation, and since I'm not asking for anything besides a few personal belongings, my lawyer thinks it should be "quick and painless."

I've been going to work normally, taking care of my cases during the day, and still working a few shifts at the diner at night. Each time I do, Keaton shows up at the start of my shift and sits at the counter until I'm done. He says he doesn't like sleeping without me, and if I'm being honest, I love it. Sometimes he brings Julian and Sawyer. Brooks has come once and has since claimed he will be back for the pancakes.

It's nice to have people.

I walk around, taking orders for the shift workers who come in for their late-night meals, and all the while, I feel his eyes on me, keeping tabs on me. It feels protective, but it also just feels like love.

Like he *wants* to be here.

I walk by him again as he stares up at the television, but as I brush by him, I feel his hand graze my ass. I turn back to him and give him a knowing look.

"Watch it, sir," I tell him. "My boyfriend is the jealous type."

As soon as I say the words, I freeze. My eyes go wide, and I stare back at him. I cannot believe I just fucking said that.

But he doesn't look scared or uncomfortable. He looks amused.

"Boyfriend, huh?" he asks. He leans back against the bar, and if I wasn't so fucking embarrassed right now, I'd be so fucking turned on. Because *God*, the way he looks right now... One arm up on the counter. Shaggy, perfect sandy locks tousled about. Muscles bulging from his tight t-shirt. And that look in his eyes...like he's starving, and I am what he's hungry for.

I don't answer him, because I don't know what to say.

That devilish smile stays on his face as he pushes himself to stand, walking toward me.

"Well, I guess now is as good of a time as any," he says, "now that I know it's official."

I swallow.

"A good time for what?"

"For me to ask my girlfriend to move in with me—officially," he says. I stare back up at him. I don't say anything. I just blink like an idiot. He chuckles and takes my hand.

The crazy thing is, I hadn't even thought about my living arrangements after Tanner. I've been so lost in all the changes, so lost in Keaton, that I hadn't even considered what my next move would be. Maybe because I'm not really interested in any moves after Keaton. He's the only move I want to make.

"Keat, are you...are you sure?" I mumble. "It's only been... I can find somewhere else, and we can... I'm sorry. I should have brought this up before. I don't want you to think that I just expected—"

He cuts me off with a long, beautiful kiss. When we come apart, he holds my face in his hands.

"I have waited long enough for you, Evie Dawson," he says. "Don't make me wait any longer. I meant what I said. Whatever is mine is yours. You are the only part about this city that makes it feel like home to me. And if here isn't home for you anymore, just tell me where it is, and I will follow you there."

I blink back tears.

The old Evie would fight him on it, would want to make sure he knew I wasn't expecting anything, that if he wanted to take things slow and casual, that that would be okay. But the new Evie, the *real* Evie, knows that she's waited long enough for someone to see her the way that she should have seen herself.

The real Evie knows that the man in front of her has loved her for years, better than anyone ever has, and better than anyone else ever could.

I wrap my hands around his wrists and smile through my tears.

"Then let's not waste any more time," I choke out. He smiles and kisses me again.

A FEW MORE DAYS HAVE PASSED, AND I am quietly humming to myself in the study of his—*our*—apartment. He hired movers to bring back a few boxes of things from the house I shared with Tanner. Tanner was there, but he didn't put up a fight.

Finding places for my things here with Keaton has been so freeing, so healing, like a lesson in bringing some parts of the past to the future with me without letting them taint it. Keaton keeps telling me to "put whatever you want wherever you want it." He says that this apartment never felt like his until I stepped foot inside it.

He also told me that if I ever bring up paying for anything here again, he will take me over his knee like he did in the pool house that night.

I've been tempted several times.

When we were kids, I never let myself become comfortable with his money. I'd run ahead of him at the fair so I could pay my own way before he could. I'd buy my own food from the food trucks by our school. I'd do anything I could to prove to him that I didn't care about it.

Because I didn't.

I didn't picture life with him in a castle somewhere far, far away.

I just pictured him.

But it's different now. Because I actually *do* live in a sort of castle with him.

And he is adamant that it's *ours*.

I'M UNPACKING some of my books onto his massive built-in bookshelves when I feel someone pinch my sides. I shriek and stumble off the ladder, right into his arms. He kisses me hard, and I let my hands roam his hair while he spins us around slowly.

"Hi," I say when we finally come apart.

"Hi, you," he says, holding his forehead to mine. We stand like this for a few moments, and I feel his grip on me tighten.

"What is it?" I whisper.

I love how in sync we are.

"Another one of the victims...survivors?" he catches himself. "I don't know what to call them. But another one of the women wants to come in and talk to us."

I sigh as he sets me down on the ground.

"I feel like a selfish bastard because my first thought was, 'I can't do this.' Imagine that. Imagine the bullshit they've been through because of my father, and my first instinct is to bitch about having to hear about it."

I take his hand and lead him toward the giant window seat.

"Keat," I tell him, holding his hand, "it's okay that you don't want to hear about it. You didn't do this.

Cato did. And he is the one who should be bearing the brunt of this. But since it can't be him yet, you and Julian...you don't know how freeing this could be for these women. Just feeling like someone gives a shit— someone who can actually do something about it. I love you for that, Keat. I hate that you're going through this, but I love that you are that someone for them. Just like you always have been with me."

He looks up at me, raising an eyebrow.

Then his lips curl up into that smile that makes me squeeze my legs together.

"Did you just tell me you love me, Dawson?" he asks.

I roll my lips together, butterflies zooming around my stomach. He leans back against the window, our fingers still interlocked. The old Evie would second-guess it. She would worry about how it may be taken. That she was coming on too strong, that she was too much, that she didn't deserve to get to share how she felt.

But not this Evie.

Not *his* Evie.

I stand up and step between his knees. I take his face in my hands, looking down at him and stroking his cheeks with my thumbs as I stare into those gray eyes.

"Yeah," I whisper, "I said that I love you, Keaton. Because I do. You are so, so loved. And when this is all over, if we need to go live in an apartment like Nanny's, I'd happily share a twin bed with you every day...as long as it's you. You deserve so much love, Keat. And I'm going to give it to you."

He smiles up at me, and I see his eyes getting glassy.

Oh, god.

I don't know if I can handle a crying Keaton. But he doesn't break fully. I see him swallow back the tears, reaching one hand up to cup my cheek. He wraps his hand around my head and pulls me down for a long, slow kiss.

"You always gave me love, baby," he says. "You just didn't realize it." He kisses me again, long and hard. I curl up against him on the seat, and it feels so fucking good. It feels like everything I went through with Tanner, and my family, all the love I was missing, was worth going through for just this tiny moment right here and any others that I get to have with him. The way he looks at me. The little smiles he is constantly flashing in my direction. The way he thinks about my every move. The way he cherishes the time we spend together.

Like he adores me.

Like I don't have to earn it.

"Eve?" he asks me after a few minutes of blissful silence.

"Hmm?"

"Will you come with me?" he asks. I turn my head up to meet his gaze.

"Of course," I tell him. I don't know if I can handle it either, but I know that I'm going to try.

KEATON

I wish I could have sat there with her in that window seat for hours—days, even. Whenever I'm with her, I find myself wanting more. More time. More laughs. More smiles. More sex.

More of her.

But knowing that this meeting was looming made it feel all the more important...necessary. Like she is my lifeblood.

We're getting on the elevator to go up to Julian's penthouse, and my heart is thudding in my ears. I swear I can hear the blood pumping through my veins. I am dreading this. I'm dreading sitting across from this woman and looking her in the eyes, hearing about all of the things my father put her through. Our legal team is here, making sure we don't "say anything that could lead to us being considered a cooperative party," which in and of itself makes me want to vomit. They're also here to discuss the compensation that my brothers and I will be giving them, which also feels so wrong. How do you put a number on something like that?

Our lawyers are still looking into that too, because paying them may be a conflict of interest and hurt the case. And if it's the last thing I do, I will bring Cato to justice.

The Everett name used to mean something.

It was synonymous with old money. A family who truly realized the American dream. And then a family who shared it. My great-great grandfather bought thousands of acres of land surrounding Bedell House and then gave them away.

My great-grandfather used to take a horse-drawn buggy around the city during the holidays and hand out stacks of cash to as many people as he could. He built affordable housing in the city, libraries, parks. My grandfather used to let us pick out an apartment building on Christmas and walk around, knocking on doors, bringing people money and gifts.

He used to tell us that "no man should starve when we got to have eight tables."

But now, the Everett name is synonymous with greed.

It's smeared by the man who raised me. The man who bought as much land as he could to protect his own view or to hike the price and make sure his neighbors were rich. The man who has never considered someone else's experience. The man who had the world on his platter and decided it wasn't enough. The man who takes advantage of everyone he possibly can and has never felt an ounce of remorse. The man who spent my whole life letting me know that I wasn't up to his standards.

And the man who made this impossible, disgusting mess. This man who has hurt so many people.

But we're going to take our name back. We're going to fix this. And when we're done, Cato Everett might still be rich, but he will have lost everything.

The doors ding open, and we walk into Julian's living room. Sawyer is sipping on a glass of water in the corner of the kitchen, talking to Russ and Tyler. Julian is seated at the back of the apartment at his extra-large dining table, deep into a discussion with legal. I take a breath, and Evie takes my hand.

I look down at her, and she just nods.

"I'm here," she says.

After a few minutes, we all gather in the living room, trying to have normal conversations while we wait for her to show. Julian's phone vibrates on the coffee table, and we all collectively hold our breath.

"Wren, hi," he says, standing up from the couch. "Oh, I understand. Yeah. Yes, we all are, but...no. Yes, yes. Whatever she...yeah. Well, would it be better if we... Yeah, okay. I'll call you back."

"What's going on?" I ask before he even makes it back into the room with us.

"She's here, downstairs with Wren in the car we sent. But she's having a bit of a panic attack. Wren offered to take her back home, but she doesn't want to leave. She's just...stuck."

We all get quiet.

Goddamn Cato. May he one day feel every ounce of pain he's put these women through.

"Can I try talking to her?" Evie pipes up, and all of our heads whip to her.

"Eve..." I start to say. I want to protect her from this as much as I can. I don't want her to be involved in this any more than she has to be. But if I learned one thing from my brother and Sawyer over these last few months, keeping the people who love you at bay doesn't help anybody.

She squeezes my hand.

"I do this for a living," she says. "Plus, I know a thing or two about being around mediocre men who think they can have and do whatever they want."

We all look at each other. Julian looks to me, but I look back at her.

"If anyone can do it, it's you, baby," I tell her. She smiles.

"Okay," Julian says. "Let me call Wren."

He steps out of the room for a second, and Sawyer looks at Evie.

"You got this," she says with a wink. Evie beams at her.

"I'm going to do my best," she says. Julian covers the bottom of his phone and nods at us.

"She said she would give it a go. You can go down," he says.

I draw in a long breath.

She steps up on her tiptoes and leaves a short, sweet kiss on my lips.

"I'll be back," she says. I nod, and then I let her go. Talking to people, getting to know people...it's one of Evie's gifts. It's the reason I fell in love with her all those years ago. Not just how she does it with me, but how she does it with everyone else. The way she can meet someone and know their life story in ten minutes. How she finds basic connections with humans based off their coffee order or the concert t-shirt they're wearing.

I knew she would be a phenomenal social worker. Because where some people run away from hard things, she runs *to* them. She runs in the direction of the danger. In the direction of the difficult. In the direction of the people who need someone like her in their corner.

And as much as I hate the idea of sending her off to undoubtedly get to know this woman and to immerse herself in the mess that my father has made, I know I need to. For Ally. For the case. For my brothers. And for me.

Evie has been through so fucking much. But she was right about one thing. No one has ever known me or loved me the way she has. And I'm going to let her do what she does best.

I watch as she gets on the elevator and wave as the doors close, taking my heart, my soul, everything I have with her.

EVIE

The ride down to the garage level feels like it takes forever, but I use that to my advantage. I slow my breathing down, trying to calm my own nervous system down before I talk to her.

Ally.

I don't know a single thing about her other than, at some point, Cato Everett hired her, wreaked havoc on her life, and then either did away with her like she was disposable or made her life so miserable that she had to leave herself.

Oh, and I know that she's twenty-four.

I take in one more breath as the doors open into the garage. Todd is waiting for me outside the black SUV. He opens the door, and I slide inside. He closes the door to give us some privacy but stays right at the perimeter. I hear the doors lock. I turn. In the way back is a woman with long, black hair pulled back into a perfect pony. She's wearing jeans, a blazer, and has some super-cute heels on. Her look says "all business," but the way she is clutching onto the hand of the other woman in the car says that she's a girl's girl. She's not letting go.

In the seat next to me in the middle row sits a woman who looks scared shitless. She has a short blonde bob that's pulled back into a clip, but the front pieces have fallen out and are daintily framing her face. Judging by her tear-stained cheeks, I'm going to guess this is Ally, which would make the other woman Wren, the journalist.

"Ally?" I ask. She looks up at me and nods her head slowly, sniffing. I stick my hand out.

"I'm Evie," I tell her. "Thank you for letting me come down."

She doesn't say anything, just nods. I turn to the back.

"And you must be Wren?" I ask. Wren nods slowly but looks a little unsure of me, which is definitely fair because based on the knowledge she now has of Cato and the inner workings of the company, I wouldn't trust an Everett or anyone close to them if I were her. I smile at both of them.

"It's really nice to meet you both," I say.

"Thanks for coming down," Wren says. "We're just having some trouble getting out of the car. I let her know that I'm happy to take her back home. She doesn't have to do this. We're just thinking things through, I think," she says, reaching up to pat Ally's knee. I smile and nod.

"I get that," I tell her. "Ally, I just want to start off by saying that I don't know your whole story. But I don't need to. I just want to let you know that I am so sorry about whatever has happened to you. And that even if you never step foot in this building, you should be so proud of yourself for getting in this car and even coming down here. That's a huge step."

She looks up at me briefly, nodding slowly, then her eyes drop to her lap again.

"The man who did this...the man who hurt you, I have known since I was fifteen years old." At that, her eyes flick up to me. I choose my words carefully. Technically, these conversations are supposed to be off the record, but I still can't say anything disparaging. I won't hurt Keaton any more than he's already been hurt. "I know that when a man has power over you, it can be incredibly hard to convince yourself that you have any at all. But I want you to know that those men up there..." I say, pointing up into the building, "those men up there are good, decent men. I've known them since I was fifteen too." She just stares at me. I clear my throat and go on. "Not too long ago—actually, very, *very* recently—I was in a situation where a man had a lot of power over me. So much so that it felt...dangerous. And Keaton Everett? He's the man that showed me I was strong enough to get out of it. He gave me a safe place to land. But most importantly, he told me—and has reminded me, over and over again—that none of it, not a single part of it, was my fault."

I see her eyes start to fill with tears. She bites her

bottom lip as her eyes narrow on mine. I reach out and take her free hand. She flinches slightly, but then she turns her hand and locks it in mine. "So I am here to tell you that no matter what happened to you, no matter what decision you make tonight, no matter how you decide you handle this...none of this was your fault. None of it. And whatever decision you make has to be the right one for you. No one else."

She sniffs again, nodding slowly. She blinks, and tears fall from her eyes.

"I'm sorry about what happened to you too," she says, looking up at me. Then she looks at Wren. "I think I want to try to talk to them."

Wren smiles softly and nods. We get out of the car, and Russ escorts us to the elevator. When we get inside and the doors close on us again, I feel her stand closer to me and take my hand. Before we get to the penthouse, she turns to me.

"Will you sit with me?" she asks. I turn to her. "While I talk to them. I think I...I'd just like it if you were there."

I squeeze her hand.

"Of course," I tell her. "Wherever you want me to be, that's where I'll be. And if you need a minute, you let me know. I'll kick all those rich pricks out."

At that, she actually cracks a smile, and Wren snickers next to her.

Finally, the doors ding and open. When we walk in, the only person waiting for us is Sawyer in the living room. I smile at her.

Women really are the fucking best.

"Hi," she says calmly. "I'm Sawyer. I'm Julian's fiancée."

Ally waves shyly, and then Sawyer and Wren shake hands.

"The guys are up in the study," Sawyer goes on, "but we thought maybe you would feel a little more comfortable if you got your bearings before you had two Everetts staring back at you." She gives a little nervous giggle, and to my relief, Ally does too. They are about the same age, so it was smart for Sawyer to be out here waiting. Another person in Ally's corner.

I turn to Ally.

"What do you think?" I ask her. "You ready?"

She nods quickly, and then we lead her through the penthouse and up the floating stairs.

"Is the other brother still not here?" Wren asks as we make our way up. Sawyer and I flash each other a look.

"Unfortunately, no," I tell her. She nods slowly.

"He's...uh, he had a conflict," Sawyer adds. Wren scoffs behind us.

"I wonder what could be more important than the future of his family?" she adds coyly under her breath. Sawyer and I shoot each other a look as we get to the top of the steps—because we've been wondering the same damn thing.

We walk down the hall, and I knock on the study door.

"Come on in," Julian calls, and we all take a collective breath and walk in, Ally's hand still with a death grip around mine. As far as I'm concerned, she can break my fingers right off, because I'm not letting go until she does. When we walk in, Keaton's eyes find me like magnets. His eyes are on me and me only. He's surveying the situation, making sure I'm okay, then moving his gaze to her, taking her in and seeing how she is acclimating.

Julian speaks first, moving slowly across the room toward us.

"Hi, Ally," he says, his voice low and gentle. "I'm Julian, and this is my brother, Keaton. I'm sorry that Brooks couldn't be here tonight. But our legal team will be filling him in on anything necessary."

Ally nods as she shakes both of their hands, and I watch as Keaton takes hers. He looks deep into her eyes, and he gives her a swift smile.

"Hi, Ally," he says. "I can't thank you enough for coming here to talk to us."

She nods slowly, and he stands to the side so Julian can lead us to the sitting area inside the huge study. It's a crystal-clear night, and you can see the entire city from this room. Ally sits on the larger couch, and Wren and I flank her. Julian waits for Sawyer to sit in one of the chairs and takes the one next to her, Keaton taking the other.

"Can we get you anything to eat or drink?" Julian asks. Ally clears her throat and shakes her head.

"No, thank you," she says. He nods then claps his hands and leans forward.

"Ally, I just wanted to start this off by saying how sorry my brother and I are for what has happened to you. A member of our legal team will be joining us, but she will just be taking notes. If you want to stop at any time, or if there is anything you don't want to get into, you just let us know. Whatever you want to tell us, we are here and ready to listen. Just as a reminder, anything said in this room is confidential until this is brought to court."

She swallows and nods.

"I understand," she says.

I pat her hand, and she scoots closer to the end of the couch.

"Well," she says, "I got hired as an assistant at Everett Enterprises three years ago."

"Okay," Julian says, "and who hired you?"

"A man named Larry Cramer," she says. Keaton and Julian shoot each other a look.

"Did you go through HR at all during the process?" Keaton asks. She rolls her lips together and shakes her head.

"No," she says quietly. "I realize now that I probably should have thought about that. That was pretty stupid of me."

I squeeze her hand, and she looks at me.

"None of this is your fault," I repeat to her. Her eyes are wide, and she nods.

"I had applied for another office assistant position and got a call from Larry himself, saying they were really impressed by my resume, and could I come down to the office for a quick interview. I was scheduled the following day, and Larry met me in the lobby and brought me back to the conference room. I ended up meeting..." She pauses for a moment. "I ended up meeting Mr. Everett that same day. The interview was only with him and Larry. They asked me a few questions and then offered me the job within minutes."

Julian and Keaton stay calm and collected, but I know Keat. I know his blood is boiling in his veins.

"Do you happen to remember any of the questions they asked you?" he asks her.

She thinks for a moment.

"It was a lot about how old I was," she says. "Not really about my prior work experience, but my age. And then they asked me what I liked to do for fun, and if I would be willing to work nights and weekends. When I said yes, they offered it to me. They also paid me by check every two weeks, but the money came from another account, not Everett Enterprises."

She looks up at Julian.

"Again, I should have thought... It was my first real job out of college, and I just really needed the money. They told me that I was being hired under Mr. Everett's personal account, not by the company, and I just thought..." She pauses for a minute, rubbing her temple.

"Hey," I say, "this is *his* fault. Not yours."

Keaton clears his throat and scoots toward the edge of his chair. He looks right at Ally.

"Ally," he says, and her eyes flick to him, "Evie is

right. You didn't do anything wrong here. I just want that to be out in the open, that no one in this room thinks you are responsible for anything that happened."

She nods slowly, and he nods back.

"Okay," she goes on. "I started working the following week. At first, it felt fairly normal. A lot of scheduling of meetings. My office was in the same wing of the building as Mr. Everett's suite, so I was pretty separate from the rest of the employees. He gave me my own parking space in the private garage with his car, and I had my own key card to get in the executive entrance of the building. I was..." She lets out a sad laugh and shakes her head. "I was actually pretty excited about it at first."

I squeeze her hand, and Wren puts her hand on her back.

"A few weeks into it, he asked me to join him for a board dinner at a hotel nearby. He asked if I could come to take notes. It was late at night, around ten, and he told me to 'wear something that showed off my age.' And you know what? I did."

"It's okay, honey," Wren says to her. She sniffs, and the tears start to stream down her cheeks. I start to worry that this might be too much for her, but she keeps going.

"That night, we ended up in this massive penthouse suite at the Landry Hotel downtown. It started off with dinner then drinks. Then a few of the board members started leaving, then a few more, until it was just Mr. Everett and one other board member." She bites her bottom lip to keep it from quivering. "His name was Rocky Breckard."

Julian and Keaton flash each other another look, but this time, they look confused. Like maybe they don't know who this guy is.

"Rocky spent the next few minutes rubbing my shoulders, telling me how 'tight' my body was, and telling me I could model. I thought he was just drunk, until Mr. Everett got up to leave. He pulled me aside and asked me if I could do him a favor."

She pauses again, and it feels like the room is so quiet that I can hear my own heartbeat. Finally, she collects herself and goes on.

"He asked me if I could 'make Rocky more comfortable.' He said he had flown in from Miami, and they were close to reaching a deal. He was pretty sure that if I threw myself into the ring, he could get Rocky to close it."

Her voice cracks, and I throw my arm around her.

"Oh, sweetie," I whisper.

"Do you want to stop?" Wren asks her. But she shakes her head.

"No," she says. "I need to say this."

KEATON

I feel sick. I feel physically ill. But I keep my eyes trained on her. I try to keep my body language relaxed so I don't make Ally uncomfortable, but I am grasping here. I want her to go on. I need her to finish her story. But in the same breath, I want to cover my ears and run away like a child.

Just as my leg starts to bounce, I feel a warm hand on it. I look down at Evie's perfect hand clutching onto me, her other arm wrapped around the brave woman in front of us. My eyes meet Evie's.

"I'm right here," she mouths. I nod subtly then fix my gaze back on Ally.

"I...I felt like I couldn't say no," she says. "I felt like if I told him no, I for sure would have lost my job. But there was also something...maybe the fact that I felt so alone? I don't know. There was something that told me that even if I said no, the answer would still be yes. So I did it. Mr. Everett left the room, and I had...I sealed the deal with Rocky. When we were finished, he left two thousand dollars cash on the nightstand. I left it there and ran. I have never felt that unimportant in my entire life."

Evie wraps her arm around her tighter. Ally takes a break and lets slow, quiet sobs run through her body before she collects herself. I have the urge to reach out and hug her too. But I get the feeling that the last thing she needs is another Everett man initiating physical touch without her consent. So I just sit here quietly. Julian and I catch each other's eye several times. And we keep listening. We listen to her tell us how this happened more than a dozen times over the course of the year with more than a dozen different "colleagues" or "board members," none of whom are actually employed by Everett Enterprises. Then one fucker got too rough with her, and she threated to go to the police. Cato let her leave, but reminded her about the motherfucking NDA again. Just like he did with the first one. And God knows how many others.

After a year, she had finally had enough. She didn't even put in her two weeks. She just stopped showing up. We listen to her tell us that, a few months after she stopped working, she had a breakdown. She checked herself into a facility when she had some suicidal thoughts and that her therapist has been super help- ful. She still hasn't told anyone else in her family or any of her friends about it, because she wasn't sure how much the NDA covered, and she's been afraid.

So this woman has just been sitting on this.

She tells us how she pays for her therapist out of pocket and is still paying the bill from the hospital stay because she hasn't been able to hold down another full-time job since. I make a mental note to have money wired to her accounts as soon as possible.

When she finally finishes, Evie wraps her in a long, hard hug. She cries on Evie's shoulder, and Sawyer and Wren surround her, rubbing her back and hair. Julian and I just sit there, helpless. When they finally come apart, we all stand.

"I think our lawyers explained to you," Julian says, "that we can't offer financial help yet because it could be considered a conflict of interest for the case. But I can assure you that we will be going after financial compensation for each and every one of you. And as soon as we can figure out a way to safely do it, all of your medical expenses will be covered by our family."

She nods.

"Thank you," she says. Then, to all of our surprise, she hugs him. He pats her back gently. When she lets go, she turns to me and does the same. I hold her a little longer. I squeeze her back, letting her tears soak my shirt.

"None of this is your fault, Ally," I tell her. "And you have just helped us in making sure that he never does this to anyone else again. We can't thank you enough."

She looks up at me.

"Thank you for listening," she says, and my heart breaks. Listening. The bare minimum. That's all she wanted. Before she leaves, her and Evie exchange numbers, and I hear my beautiful woman tell her to call or text her anytime. They make plans to get coffee next week. Before they leave, Wren turns to us.

"Thank you both for doing this," she says. "It's nice to know that there are good men in the world."

"Thanks for giving us a chance to try to fix this," Julian says. She nods, but before she follows Ally out, Julian stops her.

"We have a problem," he says, then he looks back at me. "Well, another one. One of my assistants has been looking into job postings. Another assistant position was posted last week."

All of our eyes grow wide. I look at my brother, then to Evie, then to Wren.

"Fuck," I mutter.

"Yeah," Julian says, rubbing the back of his neck.

"What do we do?" I ask. "We can't let some unknowing woman walk in there and take that job knowing what we know now."

Julian nods slowly, walking toward the huge windows. He puts his hands on the sill, his arms straight. I can see the weight on my big brother's shoulders, and I'm desperate to help him carry it.

"I'll do it," Wren says, and all our heads whip to her.

"What?" I ask.

"Absolutely not," Julian says.

"No fucking way," Sawyer chimes in.

"I don't know that we really have a choice," she

says. "If we do nothing, then some other unsuspecting woman gets hired and goes through this same shit. It can't be one of you two," she says, motioning to Evie and Sawyer, "because they know you." My body recoils at the thought of sending Evie off anywhere near those fucking creeps. Wren looks at me then Julian. "It has to be me."

I see Evie rolling her lips together next to me. Then her big eyes meet mine.

"I think she's right," she says. "We know the signs of what's going down. We can keep her safe. She can get intel while she's in there. It's the only way."

I swallow. This feels wrong, but I don't know how to make it right.

I can tell Julian is running through the same process I am. He slams his hand down against the wall then pushes himself up.

"Okay," he finally agrees. Wren nods.

"We just have to figure out how to make sure I get hired," she says.

"Brooks can help with that," I chime in. "He still works in the office. He can keep any eye on you while he's there."

She rolls her eyes.

"Yeah, right. The brother who hasn't even bothered to show. No offense, but I won't be relying on him for security measures."

I nod. She's right.

She turns back to Julian.

"I'll submit my application tonight. Maybe we can

catch up next week? Figure out some tips for getting your father to pick me."

Julian nods.

"Good call. I'll give you a call," he says. She nods and walks out of the room, then Todd escorts them out of the apartment. Once we know they are safely gone, I sink back into the chair and cover my face with my hands.

"Jesus Christ," I mutter. I hear the leather of the chair across from me scrunching when my brother does the same.

"That was heavy," Julian says. I scoff.

"You're fuckin' telling me," I say. "I don't have a good feeling about this."

Julian nods.

"I know. But I am out of ideas. You guys want another drink?" Julian offers, but I shake my head. I stand back up and reach for my girl.

"Nah," I say. "I just want to go home and lie down with my woman."

Julian smiles.

"Fair enough," he says. "That doesn't sound too shabby." Sawyer smiles at him and makes her way across the room. His demeanor immediately lightens, and I can't help but smile too. I love what she's done to my big brother. She's softened him in the best ways. We say our goodbyes, and Julian promises to call me when he hears from Wren. And then Todd leads us back downstairs, and we make our way home.

. . .

BEFORE I EVEN FULLY UNDRESS, Evie has a bowl of popcorn made and a cup of tea for me waiting on the nightstand. She takes off her clothes, puts on one of my t-shirts, then climbs into bed, patting the spot next to her. I smile as I pull the comforter back farther and slide in. We finish off the bowl, and I sip my tea while she curls up on my chest. And as I stroke her orangish-reddish locks, all I can think about is her.

Not the atrocities I spent all night learning about.

Not about the predator that raised me.

Not about the women he degraded and used like he was a pimp.

Instead, I get lost in Evie's hair. It feels like our heartbeats are in sync. Our bodies mesh together so well, even when we're not having sex. She just *fits*.

After another hour or so, I hear her breathing shallow out, and I realize she's fallen asleep. She rolls slightly so that she's on her own pillow, her hands tucked under her cheek like a child, and I just stare at her.

This week, we will meet with more of my father's ex-employees whom he put through hell. And then we will start really working with our legal team to take down our father. We will figure out how to find out more information. We will build a case against him. And we will make a plan to dismantle Everett Enterprises as it stands and rebuild it from the ground up.

It might not work.

People might think we knew about it—or worse, that we were fucking in on it.

But we have to try.

I might lose everything. We might become the most hated family in the country—in the fucking *world*.

But if I have her right here on my pillow, our noses practically touching, then I can handle the rest.

I stroke her cheek with my thumb, but I freeze when her eyelashes flutter.

"What's wrong?" she mutters, her eyes closing again. I don't answer her, waiting to see if she falls back to sleep. But those green eyes flash open. "Hmm?" she asks again. "What's wrong?"

"Go back to sleep," I whisper, leaning forward to kiss her forehead, but her eyes stay trained on me.

"Not until you tell me what's on your mind," she says. I sigh. She's relentless.

"You are," I tell her. She blinks a few times, clearing the sleep from her eyes.

"What about me?" she asks. I lift my hand back to her face, stroking her cheek again.

"Before you came back to me, I had given up on trying to change the world, Eve. It felt impossible. It felt like, no matter what I did, people were still suffering. It was too much. Too big. So I zoomed in. I focused on smaller things. Things I knew I could take on. But since I've been with you again...you make me feel less scared. You make me feel like I can handle the big stuff again."

She smiles against my hand, turning her head to kiss it.

"You can do anything, Keat," she says. "You are changing the world every day. And the little stuff matters too. Ally is just one person, but you are going to make her life so much better. One person is still one person. One neighborhood, one town. It all matters. And the things you do are important," she says. God, I love her. "And even if nothing you ever did ever worked again, you changed my whole world."

I smile at her, staring at her in awe.

"How did I do that?" I ask.

"You became it."

KEATON

*I*t's been a week since we met with Ally, and frankly, I feel like I've been running a non-stop marathon since then. Working late nights to get everything done for my businesses back home, reading through files from Wren during the days.

I've been running myself ragged for the past week, and I'm feeling it.

I'm sitting here in my office, finishing up a few emails when I hear my door creak open. She pads across the floor wearing one of my sweatshirts, and instantly, my whole body warms. I love how she looks all the time. But there is something extra special about her being in something of mine.

Mine.

She makes her way across my office and around my desk. She doesn't wait for me to finish any last thoughts or words, she just nudges me with her knee, and I roll the chair away from the desk. She straddles my lap, wrapping her arms around my neck, and pulls me into her. I inhale her. I let myself melt into her, savoring every single zap that her body gives mine.

"Hi, baby," I whisper against her hair as I kiss just under her ear. She smiles, pulling back so that she can kiss me.

"Hi, yourself," she says, rubbing her nose against mine. "It's time to take a break now."

I rest my head against the chair, just staring at her. Letting my eyes cover every inch of her face. The big green eyes fanned by those thick lashes. Those cheekbones that make way for that devastating smile. That little strand of hair that falls over her eye. I lean forward and give her one last kiss, nodding. She takes me by the hand and pulls me to my feet, then leads me out into the apartment. We walk toward the elevator doors, and I raise an eyebrow as she nods at Mac.

"Where are we going?" I ask her. She doesn't answer, just smiles.

A minute later, we're getting into the Escalade, and Mac is pulling out of my garage.

We drive through the city streets, and she's leaned up against me, our bodies morphing together like they tend to do. Then I realize where we're going.

We pull up to Coney Island after a few minutes and hop out. Mac follows close behind us, but she takes my hand and leads me onto the boardwalk.

It's still chilly for Spring, and luckily it's later at night, so there aren't many people around. I'm still able to walk around fairly invisible. Some people recognize me, but not the way they recognize my father, or even Julian.

I wonder how much that will change when everything comes out.

We walk a little ways, her hand wrapped around my arm, our fingers clasped, and we just take in the sights. The sun is going down, there is a breeze, and the salt is thick in the air. She looks at me and smiles, and I feel my knees buckle a little. Then she tugs me across the boardwalk, and I see exactly where we're headed: the little ice cream shop we used to come to all the time.

The one where we would go on lunch breaks. Then on breaks from college Then the last time, when I thought I was losing her.

And I'd go through it all again to end up right back here. With her on my arm and on my heart.

She orders one pistachio and one cookies-and-cream, and swipes her card before I can even move. She sticks her tongue out at me playfully, then I follow her out of the shop.

"You need to stop doing that," I warn her. She rolls her eyes.

"Easy, big fella," she says. "You are richer than just about every other human on the planet. I don't think anyone is worried that you're mooching off of me."

I roll my eyes before I lunge for her arm, snagging a lick of her ice cream as she squeals.

"It's not about that and you know it," I say, licking

the ice cream off my lips. "I told you I was going to give you the world. And I meant it."

We walk onto the beach, and she pops a squat right in the sand. I follow suit, and she turns to me.

"You already have," she says. "And besides," she goes on, turning to face me, "this is *my* date. Stop trying to steal it by being all romantic."

I smile at her as I finish off my—well, *her*—ice cream.

"Do you want to know why I brought you here?" she asks.

I turn to face her now, looking down into those big eyes.

"Tell me."

"I brought you here because the last time we were in this spot, I made the wrong decision."

"Eve..." I start, but she holds her hand up.

"I just want you to know that I'm so happy that I did."

My eyes widen, but I let her go on.

"I'm so glad that I did, because even though I hit rock bottom, I get to start over now. And I get to do that with you. I have never felt so much like my genuine self as I do when I'm with you. I don't feel afraid. I don't feel limited. I feel like I can do anything. Because even if I can't, I already have everything." Tears prick in the back of my eyes, but I keep it together. She clears her throat and goes on. "Thank you for always seeing me, Keat. Even when I didn't see myself. I wanted to bring you back here to make a new memory. To reclaim this spot for us. And to promise you that I'l let you steal my ice cream for as long as you want."

I let her words sit with me for a moment. I replay them, soak them in. And then I reach out and cup her face in my hands. I pull her in for a long kiss, then rest my head on hers when we come apart.

"I have a ring, Eve," I whisper. I open my eyes, and she is staring at me, like a deer in headlights. I smile. "Take a breath."

Her chest heaves up and down a few times.

"You...you have a ring?" she mumbles.

I nod.

"I've had it since our junior year of college." Her eyes grow even wider, if that's possible. "I always had hope, Eve. Even when my head was convinced we would never happen, some part of me knew."

Tears fill her eyes, and she drops her head to my chest. I slowly lift her off, holding her face in my hands.

"Doesn't have to be now. Doesn't have to be in a year. Doesn't have to be ever, if you don't want it. I just want you to know where I stand. You said for as long as I want it? I want this, you and me, till they put me in the ground."

This next chapter of my life is uncertain. Scary. Unstable.

There are so many unknowns, except for the obvious: everything is about to change.

But when it does, I can weather it.

Because Evie Rae Dawson loves me.

EPILOGUE

EVIE

"Congratulations, Miss Dawson," my lawyer says. "You are officially divorced."

I stare down at the paperwork she's handing me and blink about a few million times. I look back at her.

"Everything okay?" she asks. I swallow and nod.

"Yeah, yeah," I say. "I just can't believe that after all of this...everything I went through...that it's finally over."

She puts a supportive hand on my shoulder.

"You deserve a fresh start," she says. "Take it."

As she walks away, like that scene from *Sixteen Candles,* I see him. He's leaning against the Escalade with a single rose in his hand. When we lock eyes, he smiles and walks toward me. When he reaches me, I throw my arms around his neck, and he takes me into his arms, swinging me around.

"Congratulations, baby," he whispers in my ear. "I'm proud of you."

He sets me down, and I smile up at him.

"I'm proud of you too," I say. He shoots me a curious look. "I know how badly you wanted to come with me. And how badly you probably wanted to bash his face in. I'm proud of you for refraining."

He laughs and shakes his head.

"I'd burn the whole fucking world down for you, Evie Dawson," he says. "But unfortunately, I will also do just about anything you say."

I reach around and playfully put my hands on his ass.

"In that case," I say, "take me home."

He smiles as we spin around, walking back toward the car.

"So," he says as he opens my door, "would this be a bad time to ask you to marry me?"

I laugh so hard I choke as we get into the car, and Todd drives us away.

LATER THAT AFTERNOON, I'm sitting in the study, reading a Kristen Granata book in the big cushy chair that Keaton bought me as a "happy divorce" gift. He went full *Beauty and the Beast* on me and gifted me his entire study. He had it repainted and let me pick out the furniture I wanted. He told me to make it mine.

I'm still getting used to the spoiling, but I'm getting there. I know that I'll never be able to spoil him in the same way, but I take pride in being the person who can bring Keaton peace. I can read him like I read one of my books. I know when things are getting heavy for him. We are so in tune with what the other needs, and I've never felt anything like it.

I hear the big, tall doors open, and he walks inside. He makes his way to my chair, and I put my book down so he can kiss me. He sits down on the floor in front of me, crossing his arms on top of my lap and laying his head down. I run one hand through his perfect hair, massaging his scalp while I read.

"So," he says, "have you given it any thought now that you're a single woman?"

I shoot him a look, my eyebrow raised.

"Given what any thought? And I'm single now?" I ask him. That makes him sit up straight.

"Fuck no," he says. "You'll never be single again. I mean *unmarried*." I laugh. I love how territorial he gets over me.

"Have I given what any thought?" I ask him again.

"Where home is," he says.

I close my book, because no, I haven't given it any more thought. Home feels like this. Right here. As long as I'm with him, I'm good.

"No," I say matter-of-factly. "Have you?"

He shrugs.

"It's right next to you. So you say the word."

I lean forward and press a kiss to his lips.

"This feels like home to me," I tell him. "Being here with you. In the city where we met. The city where I fell in love with you the first time...and then the second. The only thing that made me feel like I hadn't totally lost you was being here. I know some bad things have happened here, but this place gave me you. But Keat, I know it's different for you. If you want to leave, I'll go wherever you want."

He smiles, tucking a piece of my hair behind my ear.

"Let's stay here in our city," he says. "Weirdly, it's grown on me over the last few months."

"Our city," I say. He presses to stand and sticks out a hand to me. I stand up, and he scoops me up into his arms.

"So, you ready to marry me yet?" he asks again as he carries me out of the room and down the hall toward our bedroom. I laugh again.

"Keaton, I can't marry you the same day I got divorced," I say. He smiles as he walks into our room.

"So tomorrow, then?" he asks, kicking the door shut behind us.

Want one more piece of Keaton and Evie's story?

GET IT HERE!

PRE-ORDER BOOK **three** in the series, DIRTY MONEY, to find out what happens next for the baby of the bunch, Brooks!

ABOUT THE AUTHOR

T.D. Colbert is a romance and women's fiction author. When she's not chasing her family, she's probably under her favorite blanket, either reading a book or writing one. She lives in Maryland, where she was born and raised. For more information, visit www. tdcolbert.com.

Follow T.D. on TikTok, Instagram and Twitter, @taydanaewrites, and on Facebook, Author T.D. Colbert, for information on upcoming books!

Are you a blogger or a reader who wants in on some secret stuff? Sign up for my newsletter, and join **TDC's VIPs** - T.D.'s reader group on Facebook for exclusive information on her next books, early cover reveals, giveaways, and more!